# HUSH, DELILAH

ANGIE GALLION

Hush, Delilah
Red Adept Publishing, LLC
104 Bugenfield Court
Garner, NC 27529
https://RedAdeptPublishing.com/



Cover Art by Streetlight Graphics[1]



1. http://StreetlightGraphics.com

# Chapter 1

"How long you gonna let him do this?" Carmen's voice is quiet, not betraying the rage just beneath her words. I let her touch the cloth to the swelling ridge along my jaw and then my nose. I draw in a sharp breath as she dips the cloth into the sink, tinging the water pink.

All I can do is lift my hand in answer. It is such an old conversation, but I have nobody else to go to. At least she will let me lick my wounds and hide until I have to go back home.

"He's gonna kill you, Delilah." Carmen's voice breaks, lifting over the truth of it. She dabs again at my face then sets the cloth aside.

Carmen is right. I know he has it in him. *I wouldn't be his first victim.* The thought is through my mind before I can catch it and shove it down. He doesn't know I suspect him of that killing all those years ago, or I would already be dead. I went along with him as if I hadn't seen him come into the bar looking wild, as if I hadn't seen the wet spot on his shirt. I hadn't *wanted* to see it. So when he insisted that he'd been in the bar all night, with me, I nodded. Even when the police asked me alone, I said he was with me. *Does that make me an accomplice?*

Carmen runs her thumbs down the bridge of my nose. I close my eyes, uncomfortable at her scrutinizing gaze. "I don't think it's broken. But you should go to the hospital."

"And say what? I was hit by a car?"

"No. Turn the bastard in. Press charges. Put his ass in jail."

I shake my head, and it swims. I reach out to steady myself. Getting rid of him sounds so easy, slipping from her mouth. I've walked through that scenario before, working out details for an escape that would never happen. I can't just go into a courtroom and let them fillet my private life for the world to see. I don't live like Carmen, bold and full of confidence. I need my doors and windows shuttered and don't want some lawyer airing our dirty laundry. I keep my voice small and my eyes turned away from conflict. Going to the police might hurt Jackson, ruin his childhood. I shudder to think of the media's headlines on our family—on the sordid life of Chase Reddick, prominent local business leader, and the accusations made by his quiet, nearly invisible wife.

Carmen wouldn't understand what's at stake. She isn't a mother. She won't keep a relationship past the first bump, let alone through a knockdown.

"It's not that easy. To just walk away." My words feel fat coming through my busted lip, past the swelling of my jaw. "We've got a son."

"Yeah, great. What is he learning? To cower or beat people."

"That's not fair."

Carmen shakes her head and moves on to work on my eye. The sting makes me swallow further protests behind my teeth. My mind reels. *What am I teaching Jackson? He doesn't know. He's never seen.* Every time a stray bruise creeps past the edge of my collar or down past the sleeve on my arm, I just tell him I walked into a door or tripped coming up the stairs or that I didn't know how that one happened. Hadn't even realized it was there. I had given him each lie with a self-deprecating smile. But he's not stupid, and he's not a baby anymore. He has eyes.

"Look. My aunt has rental property up in Blue Divide. You could disappear. He won't know where to look for you." Another old conversation, but I listen like maybe I can get away.

"How would I pay for that?" The longer I talk, the more slurred my words become. I lean against the rim of the clawfoot tub and clear my throat. She reaches for me while I push myself up, but I swat her hand away. I turn to look at her, putting my reality front and center for her to see. If I run, he will hunt me.

She is undeterred. "We'll work it out. You'll be safe."

"He'll never let me go." *I know too much about him.* "What about Jackson?"

"Take him. Or don't. But you gotta get away from that man."

The thought of leaving my son behind rolls for a second in my mind. To start over somewhere new without any connections. Jackson might move on without me as if I had never been. Chase could be a good father. The idea is seductive. I could change my name and become somebody else, maybe rent a cabin from Carmen's aunt and get a job in a roadside diner. Become invisible.

The fantasy clears, and shame washes through me at the vulgar thought of abandoning my son. I have to look away from Carmen. She doesn't have kids. "That's not the answer."

"Why not?" Her voice is strained.

"Getting away isn't worth losing my son. I can't leave Jackson." I turn away, hopeless, then catch my reflection in the mirror. My right eye closes to a slit. I tilt my chin up to study the ripped skin of my bottom lip. *How did that even happen?* Either I bit it during the struggle, or he punched with enough force to break the skin. The tear isn't big, but it bled over my chin, down my neck, and onto the collar of my shirt, leaving a grotesque burgundy splotch. It reminds me of one of those inkblot tests. *What do I see in this one—a shattered life? Regret? Loss? Despair? Trapped?*

He never hit me in the face before, and I don't even know what I said or did to make him angry. The moment evaporates whenever I try to think back.

Somewhere in a distant memory, I see an ambulance outside of the little house across from that college bar. I see the paramedics bringing that boy out on the stretcher. Looking in the mirror, I can't help but think that he looked a lot like me. I shift away, sick to my stomach.

"Okay," I whisper, turning to face Carmen again.

"Okay, what?"

"I don't want to die." My eyes well then overflow. Leaving him won't keep him from killing me. It might slow him down, make me forget the death at my side, but only for a time. I collapse on the lid of the toilet, and Carmen folds her arms around me and lets me cry.

*How did I become this person?*

# Chapter 2

I wake with a start, still catching my breath. He came for me in the night and was pressing me onto the bed, his hands around my throat. My eyes scan the dim room as I search for him. The weight on my chest recedes as the shapes of the room materialize.

He isn't here. It was just a dream.

The moon hangs in the frame of the window like a thin sickle, and I push the covers back to go to it. The cool glass soothes my hot cheek. I press my forehead to the pane and look out at the street below, not seeing the cars parked as I was lost in my thoughts.

*I just want to go home.* I'm so ashamed at the thought that I close my eyes, blocking out the glow of the streetlamp. He's the only man I've ever been with. We have a son. I just wish I knew what happened. What I did to set him off.

I can't do it the way Carmen wants me to—run for the hills and spend the rest of my life watching for him in my rearview mirror. I can't just take Jackson away from his friends. High school is hard enough. He might never recover if I ripped him away from all that. He would hate me. *If I leave him behind, maybe Chase will let me go.* My mind roils, still contemplating cutting ties so I can become somebody else. I would never be able to reach out to him again. I'd be my own witness protection program.

I can't leave my son.

But I know Carmen's right. Chase will kill me if I stay.

My phone vibrates in the folds of my purse, and I leap for it. Chase's name glows across the screen as if he could tell I was thinking of him. Even though I know that I shouldn't, I answer.

"Where are you?" His voice is small, contrite. All of his rage has burned out.

"I don't think I want to tell you." My words scrape across my swelling lips, barely audible.

"Oh, babe. Let me come get you. I'm so sorry. Let me make it right."

Tears roll down my face, stinging the cut on my lip. "You really scared me."

"I know. I'm sorry. It's just all this shit, you know? I'll fix it, Delilah. I'll make it better."

I don't know what "shit" he is talking about, but I hesitate to ask. "We have to get help, or I can't come back. You understand? I think you're going to kill me." The last word is lost in a sob.

"Just tell me where you are, baby. Let me come get you."

"I don't know, Chase." I push away from the window when a man walks into the glow of the streetlight. He's looking up, his hand to his cheek, holding his phone.

I freeze when the man drops to his knees as Chase's voice comes over the line. "Please come home."

He knew where I was. He's already here.

"I know I screwed up. I know I hurt you." His sob reverberates through the phone, and I watch as he crumples in the street. "I'm such a fuckup. Come home, baby. Give me one more chance. I'll make it right." He's still folded in on himself when I step back to the window, placing my palm on the cool glass.

"Will you go to counseling?"

"Yes. Yes. Anything. Just come home. I need you, baby. I need you."

It's not the first time I've heard these words. I shouldn't believe him, but I want to. This time will be different.

"I need you too." After I choke out the words, my tears flow. I'm sick over my inability to be free. But my fear of being alone outweighs my fear of him. "Just wait for me. I'll be down in a second."

He sits up, and I can see the smudge of tears on his face, reminding me of Jackson when he was small. *They are so alike.*

"Okay. I'll wait. I love you. You know I love you." He puts his hand up, stretched toward me as if reaching for my palm on the window.

I nod, and I know he can see me. "I love you too. You can't ever hit me again. You hear me? Never."

"I won't. I promise. I'll take care of you."

I feel wrung out when I hang up the phone and retreat from the window to the middle of the dark room. *I knew he would come for me.* Running away and trying to hide was never an option. He isn't going to change. He'll hit me again.

I brace myself to speak with Carmen, gathering my purse before I step into the living room. Her laptop glows, lighting her face. I join her on the couch, sitting close enough that our legs press together.

"Hey," she says, "how are you feeling?"

I hurt all over, not just my face. "Like I been hit by a Mack truck."

Carmen eyes my purse in my lap. "What's going on?"

"Chase is here," I whisper.

"I'm calling the police." She starts to reach for her cell, but I touch her arm, stopping her.

"Listen. I have to do this my way."

"You cannot be serious. You're going *back*?" Her voice rises. "He's not going to change. Tigers don't change their stripes."

"I know, but I have some things I have to put in order before I can leave."

"Like what? Buying your casket?" An angry red splotch rises up her neck and taints her cheeks. "Come on, Delilah. Look at you!"

"Don't be mad at me. Please." I take a breath and keep my voice low, almost inaudible, in case Chase has come up the stairs and is waiting outside. "I have a plan, but it's going to take a little time."

"What kind of plan?"

"I know something. I can use it against him."

The muscles of her jaw flex. I know she's willing herself to hear me out. Carmen is that rare person who can listen without interrupting or forcing her ideas and opinions forward. She is biting her tongue now, and I love her for it.

"I can't tell you anything else, not yet. I have to do this my way."

"You should run." There is fire in her voice.

"He'd find me."

She shakes her head even though she must know the truth of it.

I give her my best version of a smile, under the circumstances, and gather my purse. "I have to go."

She slams her laptop shut, gets up from the couch, then heads into the kitchen. "He is going to *kill* you. Do you not understand that?"

I'm right on her heels. "Hush, please," I whisper, pointing to the door. "Trust me. I know what I have to do."

She shakes her head stiffly.

The silence grows long and uncomfortable, and she stands staring at the wall above the sink, her shoulders so rigid they look like blades. But it's too late for me to run.

"Please don't be mad at me?"

For a moment, I think she may not have heard me, but then she turns and catches me in her arms. I flinch then relax.

"I'm not mad at you, goose. I'm scared for you." She holds me with her hand cupping the back of my head. The way I used to hold Jackson when he was small and wounded.

My body shudders as tension and dread ricochet against one another, relieved she's going to let me go. Disappointed that she's going to let me go.

"Thanks for being my bestie."

"I'll always be your bestie." She squeezes my bruised body, and I suck in a breath through my teeth before she releases me. "I don't like it."

"Me neither." I try to smile, but the corner of my mouth tugs down as my effort pulls against the cut. Tears spring over my lashes again.

"He's a bad guy. You should rent the cabin."

I nod but have no intention of doing so.

The knock on the door makes us jump.

She looks to the door then back at me. "You sure?"

I blink.

After heaving a sigh, her lips compress in a thin line. We walk to the door, where she stands with her arms crossed as I open it.

"Baby." His voice is meek and tortured. The dark hollows under his eyes and days' worth of beard make him look old and worn. He stands with his shoulders hitched forward.

"Chase," Carmen says from behind me, and it sounds more like a warning than a salutation.

I close my eyes, waiting for him to respond.

"Carmen." His voice is deep, hollow.

"Let me get my purse." I say, breaking the tense moment by walking back to the sofa.

Neither of them move. Neither of them speak.

"Take care of yourself," Carmen says as I pass her and step into the hall.

I nod, but my throat is closed, and I cannot speak.

He drapes his arm over my shoulders, and Carmen closes the door behind us. "I don't know why you like her. She is such a bitch."

I look up at him, blinking. His shoulders straighten and he gains two inches of height in the movement. There he is, Chase. Less than fifteen minutes ago, he was doubled over on the pavement, weeping for me to come home.

He steers me to the end of the hall, down the stairs, and back to my life.

# Chapter 3

Three days later, on Friday, I look worse. The red along my jaw has morphed into purple, and while some of the swelling has gone down, it only makes my bloodshot eyes more noticeable.

"What if I go pick up Jack alone?" Chase says when he comes into the kitchen.

"Don't you have to work?"

"Eh." He shrugs. "We'll knock off early. Give the boys an early start to their weekend." He pours a cup of coffee from the press then leans in for a kiss.

"I don't mind going," I offer, although I'm embarrassed by how I look. We both are.

"I know, babe. But maybe you should take another day to rest? I'll pay for a spa day if you want?"

The idea of walking into Periwinkle's with my face six shades of blue makes me blanch. "No, I don't think I'm up for the spa." I lower my eyes, careful not to look at him. "I could use the day to get some things done around here."

"Well, good. That's settled." His hand cups my face, and I resist the urge to flinch. He forces me to look at him. "You okay?"

I nod, and his hand falls away. He lifts his mug to his lips and cringes against the heat.

"Have you thought about the therapist?" They are dangerous words on my tongue, but now is the time to risk it. We are in reconciliation. Honeymooning.

"Yeah. We're gonna do that. Absolutely, but I need a couple of weeks, you know, to knock these projects out. Then we'll make the time. You can go ahead and set us up if you want." He is still trying to convince me that he'll never hit me again, to win me over.

"Okay. You still want to go?"

His face softens. "Yeah, babe. I told you. It's gonna be different."

I nod and let him fold his arms around me, fighting back tears. *He lies. I know he lies.* "You better get going if you're going to knock off early."

He smiles, winks, and heads to the door.

I watch from the front steps as he lopes to his truck, where the ladders are held fast in their racks by an intricate complement of bungee cords. He waves as he climbs into the cabin, smiling that smile that means the promise has not yet been broken. My body is still warm with the familiarity of his touch, still feeling his attentions during the night, so like those early years before I met his anger. I didn't dare deny him. I can never deny him—not if I want him to think everything is fine, that I have forgiven him.

I step back inside, lock the door behind me, then wait five minutes for him to come back. I stand at the front window, looking out onto the street. I wait another minute before pulling the curtains then going down the stairs into the basement.

I hover on the last step. It is dark and dank, the concrete floors smooth, covered in a thick layer of dust. When we bought the house, Chase installed studs for walls in order to build out rooms, but we never finished them. The room to the right of the steps is lined with shelving. It's not like Chase expects a zombie apocalypse or the Chinese government to detonate an EMP, but he's prepared. When the end of civilization comes, as long as it is in the next twenty years, we've got food. He bought ten buckets of freeze-dried food that was supposed to last for thirty years. In the corner is the gun safe, filled to bursting with his stockpiles. It isn't the food or the gun safe that I came for. I look to the boxes of junk and memories that fill the room beneath the kitchen. It is cluttered, and I scan the unfinished framing before my feet even touch the concrete. Dread flows in my veins.

I check my phone again then make my way toward the egress windows, feeling watched in the dim light. An ancient wooden baseball bat leans against a man-shaped punching bag, the light catching on its curves. The hair on my body rises as I eye the weapon. A bat might be useful the next time Chase comes after me. I could stash it upstairs in the pantry. I wonder if I could use enough force to knock him out with a single crack to the head. *God. What is wrong with me?*

I push an old vacuum cleaner aside, step over a bread machine, then stoop beneath the arms of a disused Bowflex to get at the boxes stacked along the wall. Scanning the boxes labeled with black marker, my eyes land on one marked BABY. I pull it free, remembering the contents even before I break the tape. It still smells of Jackson. I push past the quilt, the afghan, and the stuffed rabbit that he carried until he went to pre-K and decided he was too big to play with stuffed animals. My fingers graze the leather binding of his baby book, which I dig out. I cried while packing this box because Jackson was growing up and I'd just had my second miscarriage. Now I understand that they were a blessing, really—those losses. Trying to find an escape route is complicated enough with just Jackson.

My heart tugs, remembering that day, remembering my heartache. As I packed, I'd dropped his baby book. When I picked it up, I snagged the cover, and the interior pages wafted. Out fluttered a note I'd hidden away.

*You were the ugliest chick I ever dated. I don't know what I ever saw in you. You mean nothing to me. You were just an alibi.*

The memory roils, and my breath catches. I was so trapped. Even then, I knew well enough about the devil inside of Chase. Recognized the little four-step we were doing—the building tension, his explosion at me, the apologies and honeymoon period, followed by the calm that sometimes lasted for months or only for a day. His level of contrition correlated to the degree of my injuries. *How much time has my busted face bought me?*

I flip through the pages, not pausing on the photographs or my notes, skimming past my small stories about Jackson. My stomach clamps when I find the folded paper, tucked deep in the crease of the binding. I pull it free and stand to my full height, letting the words cut through me again even before I unfold the sheet.

It doesn't hurt the way it did that first time. It almost doesn't hurt at all. I set the note aside, repack the baby book into the base of the box, then reposition the rabbit and the blankets, leaving the contents the way I found them. Not that Chase would notice. He probably doesn't even know the box is down here.

Next, I reach for the box from my childhood and let it fall onto the concrete floor. My senior yearbook. That's all I need. I break through the tape and riffle through the contents. I've been racking my memory, trying to think of the kid's name. I knew it once, but somehow, it has slipped from my mind. When I see his picture, I'll know.

Mike. The name appears like magic inside my head. *Mike what?*

I fold the flaps of the box back together, hoping Chase won't know that it used to be taped. Squatting, I rest the yearbook on the top of the box to scan each page of senior pictures, printed in full color. I see Chase, his then best friend, Tom Lassiter, Carmen, me, and a hundred other people that I barely remember and wouldn't know to speak to.

Michael Dietz. The name erupts in my mind as my eyes find him. He is dark haired and thin, the sprout of an immature mustache on his upper lip. I didn't know him personally. I went to Drake for just one year, after my mom died, and hadn't been interested in making friends. I just wanted to get through it so I could get away. He was on the auto-mechanic track, and I was on the track out of town.

*I guess we both got sidelined.* He died, and I ended up right back where I started.

I remember seeing Chase around Drake High School, so when I ran into him after I started college, he seemed familiar. We had a brief affair my freshmen year that left me infatuated for months even after he had moved on. When he showed up three years later, telling me he had missed me, I was more than willing. All it took was for him to want me.

I pick up the note and slide it into the yearbook. I was his alibi. I didn't understand what he meant when I first read it, but over the years, the line stayed with me. I slowly began to see that night for what it was. I lied to everybody, saying he was at the bar all night. I thought I had won something when he came up to me, and him missing me was enough to cover for him. When he said he wanted to give us another go, I swallowed it, hook, line, and sinker. Stupid little fish.

I return the box to the shelf, wiping my hand across the top of the rest of the stack. Maybe I should break the tape on them all in case he comes looking. Instead, I go up, find a roll of packing tape, and retape the two boxes I opened. Better safe than sorry.

As I step back to examine my work, my hip brushes against the bat. I scramble but am too slow to keep it from clattering to the concrete. Heart hammering, I cover my ears as if that will make the noise less.

"Shh," I hiss at it, which is ridiculous, but I say it again.

The bat spins slowly, the block initials O.W. carved into the knob, rolling, rolling, rolling.

"Ow," I whisper to it, feeling a kinship between us. I understand how it feels to be knocked down.

My nerves are completely shot. I have been away from the windows for too long. There is no way for me to know that he hasn't driven back to the house. I don't know if I can hear the garage door from the basement. If he forgot something and headed home, I would be caught red-handed with that damn yearbook and his love note.

I crouch, terror overwhelming me as I picture him standing at the top of the stairs. *Breathe in, breathe out.* My fists unclench as I repeat the breathing exercise, and the bat slows to a stop. Opening my eyes, I see the disturbed grime on the cement where the bat rolled, the trail of my footprints coming from the stairs to the boxes. I leave the yearbook on one of the crossbeams and pull myself together. If I went straight upstairs, I would have left my footprints in the dust.

I need an excuse for coming down here. My eyes land on the punching bag. Chase might accept that I've decided to get into shape. Or he might just think I am trying to learn how to punch. *Would that cause a fight?* I drag the punching bag out of the clutter, shuffling my feet against the weight of the sand-filled base. I find my stance and punch the bag a few times, letting my feet move against the impact, stirring up more dust.

*Mike Dietz.* The name rolls in my head, and I see him being wheeled to the ambulance. He hadn't been dead then, but he was knocking.

Knowing the dead boy's name makes it real. *How did I marry a murderer?*

# Chapter 4

"Hey, I'm heading up to the store. Is there anything you need?" I called him from my car, still sitting in the driveway. I've not yet cranked on the engine, and the heat builds while I scan Bruce's house across the street. Soon, he'll come out and ask if I am having car troubles. I know he is watching. He always is.

"Mouthwash. I might be low on shaving cream too."

"Okay. I'll pick some up."

"You sure you want to go to the store?" he asks, his voice just a hint quieter, lower.

"Yeah. I've got my Jackie O glasses," I say and glance up into the mirror to take in the effect. I used concealer on the worst of the bruises, and under the shadow of the ball cap, I almost look like a normal person.

"Well, if you think you have to."

I sense his disproval and close my eyes, leaning back in the seat. "I didn't shop last week. We're pretty low. I'll go to the other store." I feel sick, plotting with him to hide our ugly truth.

"Whatever you need to do." The edge in his voice is sharp.

"I don't have to go, I guess. We could order pizza tonight, then I could wait till tomorrow."

"I think that would be better, don't you?" His voice is softer now, but that does nothing to ease my anxiety. Not when I can't leave.

"Yeah. Probably." A lump the size of a grape rises in my throat and nearly chokes the words. "I'll just wait."

"Good plan."

I nod but can't speak.

"All right. We'll order pizza. Jack will like that," Chase says, sounding satisfied.

"Yeah. Good idea. What time you going to head up to get him?"

"Probably eleven." The worksite sounds filter into the background of his call. Orders are called out, nails struck, and a saw whirs.

"Sure you don't want me to go?"

"Nah. It will give us some guy time."

I make one last feeble attempt, making my voice small, plaintive. "I just feel bad, you having to make that drive and knocking off work early. Will it put you behind?"

"We're fine, but look, I gotta go. Okay?"

"Yep. See you tonight." I sit in the car for another long minute before gathering the yearbook from the passenger seat. Me asking about grocery shopping was just an excuse to get the yearbook and note out of the house. I was going to take it to Carmen, let her hold onto it, but I can't take the car now.

The front door of Bruce's house pushes open, and he lingers on the stoop for a minute before starting down the steps.

"Heya, Bruce!" I push the door open, dropping the yearbook down onto the shadows of the floorboard.

He stops on his sidewalk. "You having some car problems?"

"No." I smile, waving away his worry. "I was going to run out to the store but think we are just going to order pizza."

"Just thought you might need some help." He nods then pauses to look down the road.

"Nah. Everything's fine." Laughter rolls out of me and across the street, and I wonder if he can hear my anxiety.

Bruce doesn't appear interested in laughing with me. He gives another quick nod then retreats up his front steps. I lean into the car and collect the yearbook, folding it against my chest as I walk into the house.

Back inside, I watch Bruce settle on his front porch, rocking. He's just an old man, but I hate him for giving regular updates to Chase about my comings and goings. I swear he thinks Chase is his son. I take the yearbook and put it high up in the kitchen cabinet above the microwave. It lies flat, invisible. Hidden in plain sight.

I set to cleaning the house, working my way through the kitchen, the living room, then down the hall to the bedrooms, vacuuming, dusting, and clearing away clutter that has accumulated the way I said I would. Worry gnaws at my stomach. Chase could open that cabinet looking for something else and find the yearbook. But he doesn't usually go snooping around the kitchen. Until I can get it out of the house, I'm at a standstill. All I can do next is find out more about Michael Dietz. No. I need to find out about the kid they put in jail for killing him.

At quarter after eleven, Chase texts that he is heading out.

*Okay. I think I'm going to lie down for a bit,* I text back and wait on the sofa, feeling the itch of flight in my feet.

*Good idea. Should be home by three.*

*Okay.*

I shift, feeling caged, and open a new browser window. *I just have to type Michael Dietz in the search bar.* My finger hovers over the screen until it goes black. I drop the phone on the coffee table, frustrated. Chase will see it. He always checks my phone.

The first time I met the devil that lives inside of Chase, I had used the internet to look up a friend from college. Jackson was three. It wasn't terrible, looking back. He had shoved me into a cabinet. My finger rises and touches the ridge of the scar that interrupts my eyebrow. Chase was convinced that I was cheating on him or looking to cheat. I wasn't. I was just curious about what happened to the people I went to school with and how I fell off the track of a career. I had a job before Jackson was born, but then we thought I should stay home with him to keep him out of daycare. When he went to school, I tried to talk Chase into letting me work as a teacher's assistant there, but he thought it was too soon. Somehow, it was never the right time. Now it's too late.

I've wasted an hour. I collect the yearbook from its hiding place and shove it into a string bag. I call Carmen as I am walking down the stairs to go out. "Hey," I say when she answers, "you busy?"

"I'm at the pool. Want to come over?"

"No, I can't. Chase went to get Jackson, and I have something I have to get out of the house."

"Okay," she says. Somebody splashes into the pool with a shout.

I stammer and stall until I am out of the house, and finally, I ask her if she will meet me at the CVS.

"I can do that. Are you okay?"

"I'm fine. I'm walking, so it will take a minute." I cut through the backyard and turn left down the alley to avoid Bruce's watchful gaze. The Flannigans, who live in the house to the left of ours, keep an eye too. They are Chase's people, not mine. I have no people. Except for Carmen.

I duck past the Flannigan's house and come out on Melrose Street, heading north, keeping my face low, shielded by the cap. I walk past two other pharmacies before I stop at the CVS. My eyes are drawn to the display of burner phones beside the jailed cigarettes.

"Can I help you?" the clerk asks when I linger.

"Do these phones have internet?"

"They can if you pay for it."

"How's that work without a contract?" I pick up a phone from the display that looks like my regular one. I consider it a moment before setting it down. Chase is never fooled.

"They're prepaid," the clerk continues. "You pay for the time before you use it, and when you run out, it's done."

"Genius." Light floods my mind. The clouds begin to clear.

She explains that I can pay for minutes through the app or come into the store and pay cash. Any store that sells the phone can do that. "So you won't get stranded somewhere and not be able to make a call."

My regular phone rings, vibrating in my hip pocket. I jump, drop the burner phone, then scuttle away from the display. I put a finger up to the clerk as I walk quickly away to answer.

"Hey," I say, hearing the panic in my voice.

"I thought you were taking a nap."

"Yeah, I was." *Should I tell him he woke me?*

"What you need at the drugstore?"

"What?" I stop in my tracks, and my breath stalls in my lungs.

"You're at the drugstore. What did you need?" His voice is conversational, not threatening. I lift my face to scan the store, searching for him. *Does he have somebody following me? Is he listening to my phone calls?*

"Oh. I need tampons." It's the first thing I think of. I turn toward the feminine hygiene aisle to grab a box from the shelf and pray he doesn't remember when my next cycle is due.

"Did I knock something loose last night?"

I wince at the pride in his voice. "I guess so."

He chuckles, and I relax, clutching the tampons like a lifeline. *This will work.*

"You're heading home now?"

"Yes. I just have to pay."

"All right. Pick me up some mouthwash since you're out anyway." The edge in his voice returns. If he's not angry, he's at least annoyed. The clouds inside my head scud closed, the way out I glimpsed when thinking about the burner phone a distant illusion.

I hang my head. "Oh, good idea. I'll do that. Love you."

"Okay." He disconnects, and I slide the phone back into my pocket, my stomach churning. I make my way to the counter, the tampons and mouthwash like headlamps lighting my way. I pause at the phone display to pick up what I dropped, but the clerk has already returned the phone to its hook. I place everything else on the counter.

"No phone?" the clerk asks.

I shrug and push out my bottom lip. "I don't need a phone. I was just curious."

She nods. I pay with my credit card and leave the CVS with my bag of tampons and mouthwash. When I step into the lot, Carmen is just pulling in. Relief floods me. I almost forgot her. I join her at her car and pass over the string bag with my minute evidence against Chase.

"Your high school yearbook?" she asks, peeking into the bag. She smells like coconut tanning lotion, and the shoulder of her coverup has slipped down. "You had to get your high school yearbook out of the house?"

"Yeah. I know it sounds crazy, but just hold onto it, okay?"

"I still think you should just leave him. He isn't going to change." She looks serious, concerned.

I don't know how Chase knew I left the house, so I don't respond. "You're getting burnt," I say and want to reach out and touch her. Maybe some of her life would rub off on me with that oil. "Just hold onto that. Keep it safe."

"Okay. Whatever. Can I give you a ride home?"

I squint at her, thinking about the possibility of letting her drive me home before I shake my head. "I better walk."

"I wish you would tell me what you have planned. I could help."

"Not yet. I've got to figure some things out first. Just don't give up on me."

"Never." She winks and holds out a pinky. It's stupid, the pinky thing, but it's a promise, and we link and shake like we are children.

"I have to go." My voice breaks on the words as I pull my finger free.

She nods, and I step away from the car. I watch her drive out of the parking lot.

My phone vibrates. *You just hanging out?*

My stomach churns, twisting as if my lie about needing tampons has brought on my period, has knocked something loose. I have no clue how he knows I'm still at the store or that I even left the house. *Line,* I text back.

I was an idiot, standing there smiling like I was free to buy a phone, like a needed a phone. I *do* need that phone. There is no other way to find out about Michael.

When I reach the next drugstore, I turn in, keeping my face low, hidden by the brim of the cap. I beeline to the display of phones on the far side of the store and select the one that looks like mine. I go to the counter.

"Do you want me to help you set it up?"

"No. It's not for me, it's a gift. I'll let him handle it." I'm nervous, afraid Chase will know that I've stopped. I pay for the phone with ten-dollar bills collected from my cash back from grocery shopping. Chase never thinks anything of the grocery bill, but the ten dollars extra every week adds up. I keep the stash hidden in the bottom of my vanity drawer. I'll hide the phone there too.

# Chapter 5

Jackson was my height when he came home from camp, but he's grown since. I catch sight of him through the window, basketball raised for a shot as Chase tries to block. The ball sails free, knocks against the backboard, then slides through the net. They pause for a congratulatory high-five. He is almost as tall as his dad.

"Good shot." Chase's voice comes through the screen door, and I turn into the kitchen. They spend long hours in the evenings shooting hoops in the driveway. The sounds of their shouts and of the ball slapping against the concrete feels like something from a perfect world, from somebody else's life.

Anxiety is eating me from the inside because Carmen called an hour ago to tell me she's been approved to hire somebody for the library at her school.

"You have to apply. It's a temp thing, a couple of months, but it might turn into something more."

"Chase doesn't want me to work," I whispered into the phone, stressed to be talking about it there in my kitchen.

"So you're just gonna stay?"

"*No.* Look. I'll talk to him, see what I can do."

Carmen sighed. "I don't understand you."

"I know. I'm trying to work something out."

"Does it have something to do with that yearbook?"

"Yes, but you know I can't explain it right now."

"Okay, okay. You don't need to snap at me. I'm just scared for you. I keep trying to throw down ladders, and you keep pushing them away."

Tears sprang to my eyes at the sound of desperation in her voice. "I have a plan. I'm working on something."

"Okay. Just try not to get yourself killed in the process. This job is a ladder, Dee."

"I know. I appreciate it—I really do. I just don't know that now is the right time."

"Whatever. Apply if you get permission." Sarcasm dripped from her words.

"I have to go." I refused her bait, not needing her to knock me down more than I've already been.

"I know. Of *course* you do." She didn't say goodbye. The line just died in my hand.

I stew as I chop salad and bake chicken. It would be the perfect job. It *is* a ladder. I wouldn't have to deal with the pickup and drop-off line, and I could still get Jackson to and from school. The slap of the basketball echoes against the backboard, and their shoes squeak on the pavement.

I worry about asking in front of Jackson. Chase will be less likely to say no if Jackson is there, but he'll also feel ambushed. He doesn't want Jackson to see him being the bad guy.

I'll pay for it later if he says yes. *Is this job worth it?*

When the table is set and the chicken is resting, I call them in to eat.

Jackson sinks one last shot. Chase catches the ball on the bounce then ruffles his hand through Jackson's hair as they head toward the porch. The door closes, and I return to the kitchen, hearing their easy conversation but not catching any of their words. My mind is too full of my own words for any of theirs to matter.

Jackson enters the kitchen and sniffs. "That smells great."

"I hope it's good. Wash your hands."

As Jackson runs water into the sink, Chase waits behind him. When I catch his eye, he winks. I smile and look away, my stomach fluttering. *Why can't he always be this guy?*

I settle the last of the drinks on the table and sit. It doesn't seem possible that this is the same man who left me bruised and battered two weeks ago. My finger traces the scar on my eyebrow like it's a talisman. *Do not forget. Do not let your guard down.*

I know I can survive another of his outbursts, but the next time might be when he beats something important out of me. The next time, it might be a tool other than his fists.

Chase and Jackson plop into the chairs with enough force to cause the contents of the glasses to ripple as elbows hit the table. Their words pass over and around me but never land. Something about basketball tryouts and Jackson's shot at making the junior varsity squad.

Breasts are speared from the serving plate to be cut and doused in barbecue sauce. It's carnage. Lettuce, tomatoes, and carrots are slathered in Catalina, leaving orange smears on the plates. When their hungers are sated, Chase and Jackson lean back like mirror images, rubbing their narrow ribs.

"You know, you'll have to cut that hair if you make the team."

"Yeah. Coach already said that."

There wasn't a break in the roll of their conversation. There's been no opportunity to ask about the school library.

"Good meal, hon," Chase says as he is preparing to rise from the table.

I jump at the chance to speak. "Can I take a job at the school? It's only three days a week, eight to two."

The cacophony stills, like leaves settling after a storm.

"They need somebody in the library. I'd still be able to pick up Jackson, and I'd be home in plenty of time to get dinner on."

"That'd be great, Mom," Jackson says.

Chase's smile is stiff.

"You're usually gone by six anyway. I think it would be really good for me to be out in the world a little bit. It gets lonely here alone all day."

"So you are not happy?" He cocks his head, and I stay seated at the table, feeling the protection of it between us.

"That's not it. You know I'm happy. But I didn't think I'd never work again. Jackson's fourteen. He doesn't need me to be here all day like that anymore. I feel like it would be nice to have, um, something besides the house." My voice is small and wheedling, already cracking under the strain of his disapproval. "I just want to interview for it."

"Fine. Do what you want." He balls his napkin in his fist and throws it on his plate. "Don't you have homework to do?" he asks when he sees Jackson still standing at the door.

"Yeah. I'm heading up."

Chase waits until our son is halfway up the stairs before turning on me. "This was Carmen's idea, wasn't it?" he asks, not looking at me.

"No. She's always known I wanted to go back to work." It's the wrong thing to say. I know as soon as it hits the air between us.

"So you've been planning this?"

"No, it just came up. The regular librarian is having a baby, so it would just be for a couple of months."

Finally, he turns to me, his eyes slits. His hatred burns me. I drop my face, unable to sustain the connection.

"I won't do it if you don't want me to." My voice is so small I'm afraid he won't hear me. But part of me prays he doesn't.

"No. You go ahead. Get yourself a job, since it's so damn important to you." He turns on a heel.

I stay rooted at the table until the TV comes on and overrules the silence. It's not over yet.

# Chapter 6

My phone vibrates against the conference room table, the screen illuminating a small rim around where it lies facedown. I press the button on the side, silencing the call, but I never take my eyes from the man across the table.

He glances at the phone, and his voice falters. "Do you, uh, need to take that?"

It is the second time the phone has vibrated in the last five minutes, and I feel the pull to at least glance but refrain.

"No. No. Please, go ahead," I say, trying to assure him that there is nothing more important than this conversation. I wish I left the phone in my purse, but I had it in my hand when they showed me into the conference room.

"The position is paid out of the PTO fund, so we can't offer you a large salary."

"Carmen explained that. It's not about the money, really. I'm just ready to rejoin the workforce, and this would be a perfect opportunity to get my feet wet. I like books. I used to volunteer in the library. When my son was here, I mean." I smile. "It would be a good—" My phone vibrates again, and I feel trapped in an uncontrollable situation. "Um, place for me,"

The sense of unease left from the last interruption elevates.

"You should probably check that."

"I'm sorry, Mr. Underhill." I flip the phone up and see the number for Jackson's high school. "Um, my son's school."

"You should take it." He nods, and I realize that my indecision must be evident on my face. I cringe thinking of the impression I must be making—the kind of person who can't even decide to answer a phone call without being told. Three attempts at reaching me feels important, ominous.

Mr. Underhill nods again. I tilt my head to rest the phone in the crook of my shoulder, my hair falling free. His eyes move with it then dart quickly away, past me, looking through the window toward the front of the school. I stand, feeling vaguely disconcerted by his glance, then walk away from the table, uncomfortably aware of my hips stretching the fabric of my skirt.

I step out of the conference room and walk to the front windows. "Hello?"

"Hello, Mrs. Reddick?"

"Yes." I don't bother to correct him. My last name is Stone. I didn't change my name because of Chase. He never wanted to marry me. But at his mother's insistence, we went to the courthouse and signed the certificate completely against his will. A wave of shame washes over me—that I wasn't good enough to marry, that I wasn't the woman Chase wanted but the one he was stuck with because his mother loved our son. Geneva also demanded we have a small ceremony at the courthouse. It wasn't the wedding I always thought I would have. It was barely a wedding at all. Chase didn't speak to me for three weeks after that, as if it was my fault that his mother was stubborn.

I turn to face the glass front of the school and see myself reflected. I should have worn something else, something less sexpot and more professional. *I'm interviewing for a job working with children, for God's sake. What was I thinking?* Slacks or a maxiskirt—anything would have been better. I hope Nick Underhill is not watching me through the glass, seeing how ridiculous I am. *What a fraud!* My face burns.

"Dr. Tate here," the voice on the line continues, forcing me back to the present.

*The principal? That's bad.*

"Yes, sir. How are you? Is something wrong?" My mind reels toward the morning, trying to remember if Jackson looked off. He seemed fine when he left the house, but I was wrapped up in my own agitation, anxious about my interview, worried about the fit of my stupid skirt.

"I have your son here in my office. There has been an altercation. Of course, you know we have a zero-tolerance policy on fighting?" It's not really a question.

"Of course." My stomach plummets, and my free hand rises to my face to tug at the small, fine hairs of my eyebrow.

Jackson has a temper. He always has. When he was a toddler, he would sustain tantrums for long minutes after any other child would have been exhausted into submission. It's gotten worse as he entered puberty, less predictable. Sometimes, he just seems so angry.

"Well, you'll need to come and pick him up."

"What's happened?"

"We'll talk about that when you get here. He's in my office until then."

"Okay." The word draws out on a long breath, and I feel chastised. "I'm in the middle of an interview, but I'll wrap it up. I'll be right over."

"That would be good. Bye now."

The call disconnects, and the phone dies in my hand. *Well, shit.*

I turn and nod through the door toward Nick Underhill. He doesn't see my constructed smile because he is looking down at the table in front of him. His expression is dark, his brows drawn together. He's not going to hire me. I smooth the hairs of my eyebrow as I walk back into the room and sit again at the table.

"Is everything okay?"

"Yes, just my son is just, uh, at the nurse's office with an upset stomach." The lie trips off my tongue like a spider.

"Oh, well, I hope he's all right."

"I'm sure he is, but I do need to go and pick him up." I straighten, resolve setting my spine. It's impossible to know if an opportunity like this will come again. This is my one shot, and I'm determined. I *need* this.

"Absolutely." He nods. A flicker of something—*relief, maybe?*—crosses his face.

"Listen, I know I don't have a lot of experience to show you, but I really, really want this job."

"Penguin's pretty good experience," he says, tapping my resume.

"It was a long time ago. I do love books though." Technically, I hadn't worked for Penguin but one of their subsidiaries, Cason Street, but it had been a real job with real responsibilities. "I worked with Cheryl Buxton, the author of *The Raven's Song*."

The name-drop has the desired effect. "That was a good book."

I didn't work on *The Raven's Song*. I worked on her next two, which were well received but did not achieve the same international success as the first one. She was a known quantity by then, and everybody expected her to produce magic the way she had before.

We smile, and he closes the folder. "Well, we'll run through your background check. I have two other people to interview. I'll let you know one way or the other by next Monday."

"That sounds great. Thank you." I reach across the table and clasp his hand, folding my fingers around his.

"No, thank you." He extracts his hands and pats mine. "Thanks for coming in, Ms. Stone. Now, go get your son."

# Chapter 7

There's traffic on the way to pick up Jackson, and I take every corner just a little faster than I should. Chase gets so annoyed at my terrible driving skills, cutting people off, and riding on bumpers. The frustration of being stalled causes the happiness at Underhill's promising demeanor to wane. If I get the job, I wonder how I'll get away when Jackson needs me if he is actually sick or hurting. Chase is right. It's stupid for me to think about taking a job. I have a family. They need me.

*It's only three days a week, when Jackson is normally gone anyway.* The war inside my head wages. By the time I pull into the high school parking lot, ten painstaking minutes have passed where I dissected and replayed all the pros and cons about me working.

*I probably won't get it anyway.* I sigh, remembering all the points in the conversation where I stammered or looked foolish. But he did say he would run a background check. That probably meant he thought I was a good candidate.

*He could change his mind, though.* I shake my head, trying to rid myself of the doubts. At least I have Carmen on my side. She'll pull for me.

As the engine cools, I sit for a long minute with my thoughts. *I'm such a fraud. I shouldn't have lied about Jackson being sick. I should have worn different clothes.* I stop the downward spiral and draw a long breath in and out to find some sort of balance. *It's okay. I'll know something next Monday.*

When the first bead of sweat erupts on my forehead, I open the door as if that was the sign I was waiting for to send me into the building. My heels tap across the pavement then reach a high, clicking staccato when I step through the school doors and onto the tile inside.

"I'm Jackson Reddick's mother," I say to the receptionist behind the newly installed bulletproof-glass wall. "Dr. Tate called." I clear my throat, trying to release the tightness in my vocal cords.

"Yes, ma'am. Have a seat."

I step away from the thick glass but remain standing, looking out the front window as the receptionist picks up her handset and calls to the principal's office.

Nervous energy jangles as I relive my conversation with Nick Underhill. I hear the way my voice sounded when he said they'd run a background check, and I cringe. Then there was the way he carefully extracted his fingers from mine and patted my hand. It's embarrassing now that I see it from a distance. I shouldn't have touched him like that. It was unprofessional. He might be married and probably thought I was flirting. *God. Why did I wear this stupid skirt?* I tug it down and hope I didn't seem too desperate.

*I am strong. I am independent.* The mantra rolls inside my mind, trying to eradicate the giddy, girlish voice from my memory, and I feel the lie of it.

*I am weak. I am terrified,* the truth responds.

"Mrs. Reddick?"

Bumps form on my skin from the air-conditioning, and a chill erupts from deep in my soul. *Should I call Chase? He'll know what to do about Jackson.* But it's too late for that. I'm already here. It will be better to just figure it out and tell Chase later.

"Stone," I correct, a near whisper.

The receptionist nods, and her lips tighten. "You can come on back."

Feeling her judgment, I compress my own lips, preparing for battle. She doesn't know anything about me, or us, by the small fact that my son and I do not share a last name. Chase just didn't want to get married. It wasn't necessarily about me.

The receptionist reaches under the desk and presses a button, releasing the circuit on the door that leads into the main school. The glass and the locked doors are new, added after the last school shooting down in Florida. It's jarring, what the glass signifies, what it says about the world in which we live.

Dr. Tate meets me at his office door. Beyond him, Jackson's long hair hangs over his face. He slouches in his seat, and his legs stretch out from the chair. The posture of disrespect, of insolence, of youth.

"Jackson, I'd like to speak with your mother alone. Would you be kind enough to sit out here until we are through?" He phrases it as a question, with that uptick at the end, but all six feet, four inches of Dr. Tate does not ask questions.

"Whatever." Jackson drags himself up from the chair, his hair swinging. He stalks from the office and settles on the bench without even looking at me. His hands are balled in his lap, his knuckles marred. The white of his shirt is splattered with blood. I see his father in the shoulder-length hair, the defiance, and the torn knuckles.

My stomach heaves, and saliva billows beneath my tongue. I stare at him with an eyebrow raised in question, thinking he will at least look at me and give some clue. He doesn't. *What the hell happened here today?*

# Chapter 8

I follow Dr. Tate into his office and sit in the chair Jackson vacated. "What happened?" I'm relieved when my voice comes out steady, strong.

"Is everything... okay at home?" Dr. Tate asks, making it clear that this is his office—he will run the show.

"Yes. Everything is fine. Please tell me what happened."

"Has there been any change in Jackson's family life? Anything that would cause your son to be acting out?"

"Acting out how?" My words are clipped. My stomach is still roiling, and I am struggling to focus. It's the blood. The arc of that splatter across his shirt has me remembering all the disconnected and shattered pieces of my life with Chase.

"What is Jackson's relationship with his father like?"

"What kind of question is that? Chase is great with him. They get along great."

"I'm just trying to understand why Jackson would be attention-seeking." Dr. Tate leans forward, resting his forearms on his desk, folding his hands together. As he does, I shift involuntarily back, not quite a flinch.

"What do you mean by 'attention-seeking'?" My voice fractures in the upper registers.

"We have noticed his erratic moods. Do you know of anything he would have to be angry about?"

"He's a teenaged boy. Isn't that enough?" A nervous laugh bubbles at the end, and I blush.

"He seems angrier than the typical teenaged boy, don't you think?"

I have no words. Tears spring to my eyes, and I look away, fighting the urge to scream. "No. I don't see that at all." I have no idea what normal anger looks like. "What exactly happened?"

"Jackson was involved in an altercation this morning."

I nod. The blood on his T-shirt and knuckles told me that much. "What happened?"

"He attacked another student."

Dr. Tate's word choice, "attacked," suggests a level of violence that "altercation" does not. "Is he okay?"

"She, actually." He levels his gaze at me.

"Oh." My scalp prickles, and I shove my hands through my hair before forcing them back to my lap. It changes everything that the other student is a girl. *Oh, God.* My mind jumps to the worst conclusions. "Is she okay?"

"She will be. Apparently, she laughed at something he said in class, and he caught her in the hall and punched her."

Relief washes over me that it wasn't sexual. "Like, *punched* her?" I ask, hoping that he has used the word for shock value and maybe it was just a shove.

"Punched," he confirms, "in the face."

"Oh, God," I whisper as a prayer. My history rises beneath the surface of my skin, and I fear that he can see the covered bruises, the busted lip, and the cowering woman I am. My finger rises to my eyebrow, tracing.

"Her parents just left with her."

"I'm so sorry."

"There's more." He opens a manila folder on his desk then slides a sheet of paper across the desk.

"Jackson drew this?" It's a gun, a rapidly rendered image with smoke drifting from the nose, or nozzle, or whatever the opening is called. My mind snaps from appreciating the skill Jackson has with a pencil when I notice something else in the drawing. In tendrils of smoke, the name "Heather" is written in thick, dripping letters.

"Oh, God," I say, hearing the broken record quality in my voice. "The girl he punched was Heather?"

Dr. Tate nods but doesn't speak for a moment, giving me time to process this new information. "We take this threat very seriously."

"A threat? But it's just a drawing." I am more disturbed by the words "attacked" and "punched" than by a sketch.

"Do you have guns in your home?"

"Well, we do, but none that he has any access to. His father has a few. But they are locked up. I don't even think he knows we have them." A chill rips down my spine.

"Well, regardless, in light of recent events, I am compelled to notify the police."

"Oh, Dr. Tate. Is that really necessary? He's just a kid. Yes, he has a temper, and yes, he doesn't always know how to control his anger, but this is just a drawing."

"No, this is a terroristic threat, and we have to notify the police."

"Are you kidding me? He is fourteen years old. He is not a terror—"

"Mrs. Reddick, he attacked another student today. We have already processed his suspension. We have zero tolerance for violence in our school. Due to the severity of this attack, I've recommended his expulsion."

"Expulsion?" I force myself not to fold my head onto the desk and cry. *How am I supposed to tell Chase?* He'll take it as me accusing him. You hit me, and now your son hits girls. *Attacks.* The word settles low and uneasy in the pit of my stomach. He attacks girls.

My phone vibrates in my purse. God, Chase is going to be pissed. He might even lash out at Jackson this time. I have to run interference, to protect him.

Dr. Tate clears his throat, bringing my attention back to him. "The board needs to review his file."

"So what does that mean?" My brain is numb. "Is he expelled or not?"

"He'll have a week's suspension, with the possibility of expulsion. To be perfectly honest, Mrs. Reddick, I don't believe we are the best place for your son. But we'll have to wait for the board's review."

"It won't happen again. I promise. I'll get him into anger management, counseling, whatever it takes." *Family counseling. That's what we need.* Maybe I can get Chase to the promised therapy if it's not about him.

Dr. Tate nods. "I think that's an excellent idea. I'm glad you can appreciate that this is not only about Jackson. Other students have the *right* to attend school in an environment where they do not have to fear violence against them."

"Of course. I'll get Jackson the help he needs. Please, give us another chance. I just don't know what we'll do if you expel him."

"I think Jackson will benefit greatly from anger management and therapy, but my recommendation will stand. If it were my choice, he would not be attending our school for the remainder of this year. I recommend you consider an alternative. Clairemont Academy is an excellent school. They are better staffed to cope with troubled youth."

"Troubled youth?" My voice crescendos and cracks. I chalked Jackson's problems up to run-of-the-mill adolescence. *What if it's more than that? What if he saw something at home?* Shame and guilt ride like waves up my cheeks, and my face blazes. *Is this my fault for not leaving Chase yet?* I massage the scar on my eyebrow.

I've kept Chase's physical beatings hidden. At least, I think so. But Jackson has heard some of the words that left scars.

Once, when our son was four, Chase called me hideous. Jackson later climbed into my lap and asked what the word meant.

"Ugly, honey. It means ugly."

He looked at me, appalled, his eyes filled with tears. "That's not true, Mama. You're bootiful."

Tears well at the small flash of memory. If he were to hear such a thing now, I doubt that he would defend my beauty. If anything, he would nod at his father and offer a fist bump.

"I think maybe you are overreacting." The hysteria in my tone bounds against the walls, and I pull myself together, swiping at my eyes. *Hush, Delilah.* "He is only fourteen," I say, my voice more controlled.

Dr. Tate only turns to his computer and taps a few quick keys. He swivels the screen toward me so I have an unimpeded line of sight to the image glowing on the screen. It takes a moment for me to understand what I am seeing.

Heather's nose is clearly broken, and the areas around her eyes are already purpling. There is blood smeared across her lips, and bile rises in my throat. I can't bear to look and turn my face away, putting my hand up for him to close the screen.

My son is a troubled youth. My son is violent. My son is the spawn of his father.

I shift in my seat. "What is Clairemont Academy?"

"It's a school in Athens." For the first time, there is more kindness in his tone.

"But Athens is two hours away." My voice is so small that I am not even certain I have spoken.

Dr. Tate slides another sheet of paper across the desk, a printout of Clairemont Academy's home page. A quick scan makes it clear that it's not just a school but a boarding school with dormitories for housing students.

"This looks expensive." The uniforms alone suggest a level of tuition beyond our budget. "Are you serious?"

"Very. I suggest you and your husband spend some time on Clairemont's website and give it some consideration. The police are going to be more lenient if they see you are taking control of the situation."

"Either we send our son to boarding school, or he gets taken to juvie? We'll get him help, I promise, but this doesn't mean *anything*." I stab my finger onto the paper—*bang, bang, bang*—and the sound contrasts with the wheedling plea in my voice. My phone vibrates again.

"Regardless, this was an attack on a fellow student, and with a terrorist threat—"

"Please stop calling him a terrorist."

We lock eyes.

"I'm sorry, Mrs. Reddick, but there is no other way to view this."

"It's a freaking drawing."

He nods, but his lips are compressed, and he is not going to argue. "I've made my recommendation to the board."

"Can we appeal?"

"I'll have Jan print the appeals process. You can pick it up on your way out." The computer behind him finally goes dark, erasing the terrible image of the beaten girl. "I don't think there is much hope of success. Look into Clairemont Academy. It may be the best place for your son." He starts closing Jackson's file, having replaced the threatening drawing inside.

I rise from my chair, pointing at the drawing as it disappears into the folder. "I'd like to take that with me."

"No. I'm sorry. I need to keep this for the police report. If you'd like to take a picture of it, you may. I'm sure the police will be by to speak with your son over the next few days."

My stomach feels like lead. I have no idea how to handle this. Dr. Tate holds my eyes, unblinking, as I process the seriousness of the charges he has leveled. Finally, I withdraw my phone to take a picture of the incriminating artwork.

"Okay. We'll figure something out. Thank you for your time." I leave his office with as much dignity as I can muster, hoping he knows how little help he has been.

# Chapter 9

I glance at my phone when it vibrates again and motion for Jackson to follow me. I have two missed calls and three texts.

*Why are you at the school?*

*Is Jack okay?*

*WTF Answer your phone!*

I text, *Jackson got in a fight. I'm taking him home. I'll call you when I get there.*

We pause at the front counter, and I don't even have to ask for the paperwork from Jan. She slides it under the glass, and I swipe it up as if she has somehow caused this terrible situation.

"What is wrong with you?" I turn on my son as we reach the car. "What were you thinking? You punched a *girl*?"

He doesn't protest, and now that I've started, I can't stem the flood of words.

"And that drawing, Jackson, seriously, what were you thinking?" I slide into my seat and hear his seat belt clicking into place while my words continue to flow, mostly the same questions asked without any expectation of an answer.

Jackson seems to tune me out. He stares through the window with no hint of emotion. My words falter as I take in his callous expression, the completely unconcerned set of his jaw, and see in him the lines of his father.

A chill washes over me, and I try to resume my rant, but after a few mumbled attempts that fail to garner a response, I say, "We'll talk about this later."

Jackson blows out an amused puff of air, almost a chuckle, and I glance in the rearview mirror to see him looking back at me.

"Do you have something you want to say?" I narrow my eyes.

"Dad will take care of it."

"*That's* your answer?"

His eyes meet mine in the mirror, and I shudder. He shifts and looks down. I turn in my seat and see that he has his phone out, texting.

*He is texting!* My head is about to explode. I can't believe he thinks now is a good time to send a group chat.

"Oh, really? Give me your phone." We are forced to turn right onto the four-lane street in front of the school, only to make a U-turn at the next light to get facing the right direction.

He snorts. "You can't take my phone."

"Oh, yes, I can."

"Because I'm texting dad?" He is incredulous.

"I am not taking your phone because you are texting your dad. I am taking your phone because you just got expelled from school for punching a girl. My God, Jackson. I cannot believe you did that."

We lock eyes in the mirror, but I have to look away to pay attention to the road. When we get to a less congested stretch, I reach back and demand the phone again.

For a moment, I think he is going to refuse, but finally, he pushes the lock button and extends his arm.

I drop the phone into my purse. "Thank you."

The silence in the car is heavy.

After a minute, I try again. "Listen, this is a big deal. You are in serious trouble. Dr. Tate wants you expelled, and they are taking that drawing of yours to the police. Do you understand what I am saying to you?" My voice is harsh, and I expect to see remorse or worry on his face, but his unconcerned expression doesn't waver. I want to shake him. To make him understand that the path he is on is going to lead him nowhere good. "Violence is never the answer."

"Except when it is," he says under his breath but still audibly.

My mouth drops open and my jaw juts forward. *Oh my God. Who is this kid?*

We don't speak the rest of the way home.

# Chapter 10

The phone vibrates in my hand, and Chase's face glows on the screen.

"Hey." I walk down the steps and into the yard to get a better cell signal.

"I thought you were going to call me?"

I pull the hem of the skirt down. It's too small, riding up. *What was I thinking?* "We just got home."

"What happened with Jack?" His voice is controlled.

"He got in a fight. Somebody laughed at him in class, and he beat them up." I hesitate, not wanting to tell him it was a girl, not wanting him to hear the accusation in my voice.

It's been better. He really is trying, even though he's had to back out both times I scheduled him for counseling.

"Who laughed at him?"

"Just a kid. Dr. Tate wants Jackson expelled."

"That's bullshit." His temper is rising—I hear it in the cadence of his breathing.

As I stand near the hedge that lines the property, I wave at Old Man Flannigan sitting on his deck just in case he is looking at me before heading back toward the house. He doesn't wave back. "It's not really up to him. It's up to the board."

"Oh. Well, that's okay then."

"What do you mean, it's okay? You should have seen what he did. He can't go around punching people because they laugh at him."

"No, of course not. I'll talk to him about that. But I know some of the guys on the school board, so I can take care of it."

"Oh. That's good." It feels wrong, though, for Chase to sweep it away. It might be better if Jackson had serious repercussions for his behavior. "Dr. Tate thinks we should send him to Clairemont Academy in Athens."

He throws out a bark. "Oh, hell no. Jack isn't going to a military school. That's bullshit."

I had never heard of Clairemont before, but there's a lot Chase seems to be privy to. "How did you know I was at the school?"

"I just did." I can hear the smirk in his voice.

I don't dare pursue that line of questioning. "When are you done?"

"I'll be home for dinner."

"Okay. What should I do about Jackson?"

"I'll call him. But we'll talk when I get home." Background noise begins to filter across the line. He must've stepped away from the site to talk. "Gotta go."

"Okay." I hang up the phone and set it on the counter. The knife block is in front of me, and my eyes linger on the handles, my mind racing.

I should have left years ago. Now it feels like the chain on me is tightening. Somehow, he knew I was at the school. And the drugstore. *He's not a god, so how?*

I go to the computer and move Chase's papers from the keyboard so I can type an email to Mr. Underhill, thanking him for his time and understanding when I had to go to get my son.

*If you have any questions or need anything further to consider me for the position at your school, please don't hesitate to contact me.*

I type my name and include my phone number beneath it. I feel guilty, sending the message, but try to shake it off. Chase already knew I was interviewing. Nevertheless, I close the browser and replace his papers on the keyboard.

A heavy bass line reverberates from Jackson's room. My eyelid twitches at his blatant disrespect for the noise level. My skirt rides up, and I stew more. I have to figure out how Chase is tracking me. After I go to our bedroom to change into jeans and a polo, I return to the computer and open the browser.

My fingers hover over the keys, hesitant to touch down. *What if he sees my search?* He might have some kind of program that saves my keystrokes and gives him a report, if there even is such a thing.

Then I remember the secret phone stored in my bathroom drawer. After locking the bathroom door behind me, I sit with my back against the wall and power it on. It takes a second for it to connect to the Wi-Fi. I open a browser then type, "How can somebody track you?" in the search bar.

Results flood back, pointing at my iPhone. Does the screen light up randomly? Does it take a moment after turning it off to actually turn off? Does the power drain? If so, then there may be hidden software running on your phone.

I scan the rest of the article and turn off the burner phone before turning my attention to my regular cell. *Is it a spy?* I push the power button and wait while the phone shuts down ever so slowly. After turning it back on, I stash my secret phone beneath the debris in the drawer. My heart racing, I make my way down the steps to grab my purse.

"Jackson?" I call out, slipping my feet into canvas sneakers from the hall closet. "Jackson!"

"What?" He pokes his head from his bedroom door and looks down at me.

"I'm running to the store. Do you need anything?"

"No."

"You okay if I go?" I feel guilty, leaving him. I should be here in case he needs to talk.

"Can I have my phone back?"

"Yes." I dig in my purse, and he meets me on the steps to collect it. "Dad said he may call you."

"Was he mad?" His eyebrows draw together, and he looks at the ground.

"Well, he isn't happy about it."

He nods, takes the phone, and hesitates before turning away. "Sorry about today. I don't know what happened."

I reach out and touch his face. "We'll talk about it when your dad gets home, okay?"

He shifts away from my hand before nodding then bounding up the stairs.

Once I am in my car, I set my iPhone within view. Usually, I keep it in my purse when I'm driving because I am easily distracted, but today, I want to see everything it does. The article said that it would light up when searching for a tower or when changing from one tower to another.

Even if there isn't tracking software hidden in the phone, the GPS positioning may be enough to give Chase the general idea of my whereabouts. After searching the internet, I took a look in my contacts as one of the articles suggested. Under *Chase*, in red, it said, *Stop Sharing My Location*, just like the article said it would. I was tempted to tell the phone to stop sharing but thought better of it. If he doesn't have tracking software on it already, I don't want him to think he should add it.

At the intersection of Locust and Taft, the phone screen flickers then goes dark. I park at the grocery and go inside, keeping my screen in sight. It doesn't light again. Since I can't go home empty-handed, I walk the perimeter of the store, picking up lettuce, tomatoes, and cucumbers before pausing at the meat counter to contemplate the options. I finally settle on bone-in chops. While the butcher wraps them, my screen lights. I nearly drop the phone.

*How did the interview go?*

I relax. It's only Carmen.

*I'll call you later.*

When I get back to my car, the phone remains dark. I drive out of my way, watching for the screen to light. Finally, it flickers at Melrose and Village Park Place.

*Son of a bitch.*

I fight the urge to throw my iPhone out the window. *Traitor.* The phone sits silent and unblinking.

# Chapter 11

The printout from Clairmont Academy is sitting on the table in front of the sofa. Chase scans it then chucks it back onto the table. He stretches and places his arm over the back of the couch, claiming it. "So, I've already spoken with Mitch Donnelly, and with his pull, Jack will be back in school on Monday."

"Really? How is that?" It's hard not to be impressed by Chase's ability to get things done.

"He's a roofer, man. We give each other work. You think being on the school board pays the bills or something?"

"Do you think we need to talk about Clairemont Academy?" I indicate the sheet. "You didn't see what he did to this kid." I am careful not to say girl, afraid that the accusation would light up my face like a banner.

"Yeah, well, we're not doing that. I'm not sending my son to some military academy when there is a perfectly good school just down the road."

"Well, Dr. Tate thinks Jackson would do well there."

His eyebrows fold together, and he snorts. "You think we can afford that?"

"I can help if I get that job."

"You can help with your little librarian job?" He purses his lips, making fun. "You win the lottery or something? A place like that's probably fifteen thousand a year. Don't be ridiculous."

My face burns. I'm such a loser. *How did I become so ridiculous?*

"Well, it doesn't even matter. He'll be back to school on Monday."

I open my mouth but can't find any words. I am a beached fish, gasping on a bank. I turn into the kitchen to pull the chops from the oven.

The distance between us gives me strength to find my voice. "It seems that we need to discuss repercussions for his actions rather than just absolution." I'm relieved when my voice has weight and doesn't tremble. After chopping the cucumber for the salad, I look through the archway, knife in hand.

"What? You want to send him away? 'Cause you know he would live there. Did you even look at this? It's basically a prison." His eyebrows rack nearly to his hairline, a challenge.

"No, of course I don't want to send him away, but I don't want him beating people up either." It's the wrong thing to say. I know it as soon as Chase nods, his jaw tight and flexing.

"Maybe he could join us at counseling," I say as if I believe we will ever go.

"Like a whole family thing?" he asks with disgust.

"What he did today was terrible." My words are brittle.

"So he got in a fight. Boys fight."

By now, Jackson has come down the stairs, looking meek and chagrined. I step into the living room, still holding the knife. Chase motions for Jackson to sit next to him. The arm stretched across the couch reaches forward and ruffles the boy's hair. Jackson does not look up.

I swallow and tighten my grip on the knife, my knuckles going white. "No. This wasn't a fight. This was an attack. He punched a *girl* in the face because she laughed at him in class."

Chase blinks. Now that Jackson is in the room, I am more confident. Chase never loses control when Jackson is around. He looks at me, his eyes narrowing as he glances down at the knife in my hand. I drop my arm, letting the blade rest along my thigh. If he sees the desire, the threat, in me holding the knife, he doesn't say anything. Instead, he turns to our son. "Is that true? You punched a girl?"

Jackson shrugs and finally produces a small nod.

"Dude, you can't hit girls." Chase glances at me.

I look away as if I am just another person in the room, of no importance. As if I am not a girl he hits. I retreat into the kitchen and place the knife in the sink.

Chase is leaning close to Jackson, saying something that is lost to me when I return. Jackson nods and smiles.

"Of course, I'm kidding," Chase says to me when he sees that I have returned.

A spot of color rises on each of Jackson's cheekbones.

I concentrate on keeping my tone steady. "What did you say to him?" I want to scream, to tell him that this is not a joke, that this is serious. "What did you just say? I missed it."

Chase looks up like a deer in headlights. "Nothing. Just something between us guys."

"I want to know." The muscles in my jaw flex, and my stomach flops. For a second, we lock eyes, and I force myself not to turn away.

"I just told him that even though sometimes you may want to, you should never hit a girl." His words are precise and modulated, controlled. He winks at me, as if this is our secret.

"I don't know how helpful that is." I snort, and my hand draws up to the ridge of my brow, finding the small scar, my touchstone.

"I'm just saying. You chicks can be frustrating, difficult." Chase shrugs, his lips upturned.

Jackson is bobbing his head as if this is some great truth, as if he has some experience with "chicks" that gives him the right to nod along.

I want to pull my hair and stomp my foot. *"Chicks?"* I ask for all of womankind.

"Yeah, chicks," he says, unapologetic. "The point is, Jack, you can't act on it. If you gotta hit something, and man, I know sometimes you do, hit a wall." He chuckles, and my teeth press together until my jaw locks. He winks at me again.

*Winks at me!* I can feel the heat in my face, and my fingers itch to touch the scar, but I hold myself steady. "I don't think hitting a wall is a good idea either. You could break your hand."

"Are you saying it's better to hit a girl?" Chase's lips quirk in a half smile.

"No, of course not!" I feel spun, like I always am when Chase turns his attention on me. I fix my eyes on Jackson instead, but I remember the bat in the basement, thinking how I would like to knock Chase over the head with it. *Sometimes, maybe violence is the answer.*

I push the thought away. "We don't want to *teach* him to deal with frustration by *hitting* people." My voice is shriller than I expected.

Chase narrows his eyes like I have crossed a line.

I draw a long breath and hold my ground. "I think what I'm trying to say is that there are more effective ways to deal with your anger."

"Of course." Chase frowns.

By now, I know he is messing with me, testing how he can get under my skin. I try to stop the conversation from spinning again and double my efforts with Jackson. "Honey, I know it's tough dealing with people, but violence can never be the answer."

"That's right. Violence is never the answer," Chase parrots my words, but everything under the surface says, "except when it is."

*Am I the only one who knows what a monster he is?* The words roll in my head, and in a jolt, I remember where I heard them. Earlier today, when I was driving Jackson home. He had said that under his breath. I can't take my eyes off of him.

"Well, your mother and I can't condone violence. I think you need an outlet. I've been thinking about trying out that new Krav Maga place over on Elkhurst. You can join me."

"What's Krav Maga?"

"Some kind of karate. You know, like MMA." Chase shrugs, and comprehension dawns on Jackson's face. Even I know what MMA is, but I do not think it's what Jackson needs.

"That would be so cool." Jackson brightens, seeing the reward for his bad behavior. He exudes enthusiasm.

Guilt flogs me. I haven't been seeing him at all. He's not a kid anymore. He is closer to being an adult. *How could I have missed the fact that he needs an outlet?*

Jackson looks to me from his secure perch beside his father.

"Well, that's settled then." I shrug. Chase has taken care of everything. He's assured us that Jackson will be back in school by Monday, and now he's promised a new activity. I feel blindsided, my back stiff and erect. "Shall we eat?"

"Yeah, it smells great." Jackson hops up from the couch. They pass by me on their way into the kitchen, and Chase's hand smacks my butt.

I glance up and see his eyes on me. I smile as my throat clamps down. "I hope it's good," I whisper, surprised that I don't sound as strangled as I feel.

# Chapter 12

After we have eaten, Chase excuses himself, goes into the living room, then turns on the TV. Jackson lingers, looking down at me where I sit in front of my mostly untouched meal. Standing there, he looks so awkward. "Can I help clean up?"

"Sure."

A beat passes while we look at each other above the carnage on the table. I can see how badly he wants to say something. I wonder if he's trying to figure out how to comfort me, to tell me that none of what happened today was my fault. Or maybe he understands why some of the blame must lie at my feet. He is my child. Everything he does is a reflection of me. Of us.

I try to make my face calm, encouraging him. The words are almost visible, sitting on the tip on his tongue, but my expression is not enough of an invitation. He picks up his plate and scrapes the bones into the trash. "Dinner was good."

"Thank you." My held breath escapes in a sigh, and I push myself up from the table, deflated. I peek in the living room to make sure Chase is still engrossed in his show before turning back to my son. "I just wish I understood what happened."

"I'm sorry, Mom." There is relief in his voice, to have the words finally out in the air.

"I know." My shoulders drop, and I place my hands on the counter, facing him. "Can you tell me what happened today?"

"I don't really know."

"They said she laughed at you in class."

"Well, yeah," he says as if Heather laughing is the norm, part of his routine.

I need more to go on. "Did you get an answer wrong or something?"

"Something like that."

"So she laughed at you, then you drew that horrible drawing?"

"I guess."

"You either did or didn't." I sigh, weary from the day stretching behind and the future stretching ahead. This is like pulling teeth. "I'm not going to get mad, Jackson. I just want to understand what happened."

"She sits behind me, you know. And she just kept saying stuff after that."

"Is she a bully?" The label sounds cliché, like this is an after-school special.

He shrugs in an elaborate rolling of his shoulders.

"Did you tell Dr. Tate that?"

"No. He doesn't care."

I nod before I can stop myself. That's exactly the impression I got—that Dr. Tate wrote Jackson off, and the details mattered little. "I still wish you had told him."

Jackson turns away and puts the jar of Stubb's into the fridge.

"So you were mad when you left class."

"Yeah. I mean, I don't know if I was really mad. I was annoyed, but she's just like that. It didn't matter." He collects his father's plate from the table, and I set water to running in the sink.

"That doesn't make any sense. If you weren't mad, you wouldn't have hit her."

"I don't remember hitting her." We lock eyes, and he continues, "I know I did. I mean, everybody saw it, but I've been trying to remember doing it all afternoon, and I just can't. It's like I was sitting in class, and the next thing I knew, I was being walked to the office."

"You mean you blacked out?" I run through the list of reasons a person could experience a blackout. *Mental illness? Drugs?* I have no idea. Jackson has always been mentally stable, even with his temper. "Are you playing me?"

The injury that crosses his face makes me wish I could pull the words back. "I knew you wouldn't believe me."

"No, Jackson. I do believe you. I'm just surprised. That's all. Has that ever happened before?"

I don't *want* to believe him. I don't want him to be like his father. The first time Chase hit me, he said he didn't remember doing it. He had seen the cut the next day and asked what *I* had done. I looked at him then, still wary, and said, "That's where you shoved me into the cabinet."

"What are you talking about? I never did that," he said. When I looked into his eyes, in that split second, I knew he wasn't lying—he had no memory of his rage.

A shudder washes through me at the memory. Jackson is avoiding my eyes again. "How many times?"

"A couple," he finally says.

"Is it only when you are mad? Why didn't you tell me?"

He shrugs, and I can tell that he wishes he hadn't mentioned it.

"You aren't experimenting with drugs? I mean, I know that some of the kids are trying things, but drugs will destroy your life." I had attributed Chase's lapse in memory to the drugs.

"Jeez, Mom. No. I don't use drugs. Jeez."

"I've never talked to you about how harmful they are. I'm not accusing you." My chin quivers, and I swipe hard at my eyes. "I'm trying to figure out what I did wrong."

"This isn't about you." His voice rises in frustration.

"Of course not, but I just never talked to you about drugs or anything like that. It wouldn't be crazy for you to be curious—that's all."

"Mom, I'm not gonna use drugs. I'm not stupid." He takes the cloth I offer and wipes down the table as I finish scraping the last of the waste into the trash.

I nod, relieved. "Well, if you are blacking out, we need to know why. It could mean something. Like an underlying medical condition."

"Like I'm crazy, you mean?"

"No." I reach out to touch his arm, although every reason I can think of is encompassed by mental illness or substance abuse. Mental illness doesn't mean crazy. We all have broken pieces. "I'm sure there are any number of reasons why you would lose time."

"Dad says it's no big deal."

*He knew?* It feels like a slap in the face. "You've... talked to your dad about this?"

He shrugs. "He told me not to use drugs too." His lips are drawn down, and there is such a look of remorse on his face that I want to wrap him in my arms like I did when he was small and scraped his knee. "I didn't mean to hit her, really. I don't know what happened."

I don't dare doubt him, not now that Chase has already accepted the blackouts. But I'm not finished. "What about the drawing?"

"Yeah, I didn't mean anything by it. I really meant that Heather is the gun, not that I wanted to shoot her. It was a joke."

"Well, nobody got the punch line," I say, trying to lighten the tension. I begin loading the dishwasher, something I don't ask either of them to ever help with. There is a process to it so everything gets cleaned properly, and neither of them care.

As I set the cycle, my mind whirs, hearing again Dr. Tate calling my son a terrorist. I want to believe Jackson about the drawing, but if someone drew that picture with his name in the smoke, it would feel like a threat. I see the haunting images of the troubled boys who have gone into schools bearing guns overlaying Jackson's face. I see the vacant, staring eyes of the boy from Sandy Hook and shudder.

"Cops are here!" Chase calls, and the TV goes quiet.

Jackson and I walk together from the kitchen, and as we cross into the living room, I see the cruiser through the window, parked in front of the house.

# Chapter 13

"Oh, God," I whisper as Chase goes to answer the door. "I didn't really think they were going to notify the police."

Jackson wants to run. I can tell by the up-and-down movement of his feet.

"It's okay, honey. It's going to be okay. Sit down."

He does, folding in on himself, looking small and young.

Chase opens the door, inviting them inside. "Hello, Officers."

"Chase." The shorter officer leans into the room with his hand extended. They shake, and Chase cups the man's upper arm like they're old friends.

"It's good to see you again, Officer."

I blink. It's a small town. Of *course* they know each other. His name tag says Grant.

"I wish it were under better circumstances." The policeman nods, his eyebrows furrowing.

Chase releases Grant's hand and spreads his arm toward the room, welcoming him. "Missed you last Saturday."

I always feel like I am playing catch-up with Chase's network. Saturdays are for his softball league. This police officer must play on the same team.

"Yeah, I hated to miss."

"Well, we lost 'cause you weren't there." Chase jabs at the officer's shoulder.

Sweat prickles in my hairline, and my stomach knots. The small bonding session happening at the door makes me feel invisible.

"Well, you know why we're here?" Grant asks, cutting short the social niceties.

"Yeah, I heard there was some ruckus today. We've already talked about it. Jackson feels right bad about what happened."

"This is Kevin Delaney, you met?" Grant motions to his partner, still standing in the doorway.

"Good to meet you, Kevin. Come on in. Can we get you something to drink?"

"No, we're good. Thank you."

"How is your mama doing?" Chase asks.

Grant nods. "She's doing some better. Keeping her comfortable—that's all we can do."

"Well, you know we are praying for her." He bows his head as if literally praying.

"I appreciate that." After their shared solemn moment, Officer Grant looks up at me for the first time. "You must be Mrs. Reddick?"

"Yes, sir," I say, my invisible skin thickening and becoming opaque again. "This is our son, Jackson."

Jackson rises from the sofa and shakes the officer's hands in turn.

"Of course, we're here about the altercation at the school today. We just need to have a conversation, you know, to put in the record."

"Of course." Chase nods and settles on the sofa next to Jackson.

"I need to go turn off the sink." With that, I slip away into the kitchen. The water is already off, but I need a moment. *Chase has cop friends.* When I think about how I planned to go to them about Michael Dietz, my knees go weak. I dodged a bullet.

When I return, Grant is standing at the fireplace, and Officer Delaney has settled on the love seat, leaning forward, as they listen to Jackson.

"I never meant to hit her. We were sitting in class, and I said something stupid."

"What did you say?" Grant is in charge, handling the questioning.

"Teacher asked who wrote the Declaration of Independence, and I know that's Thomas Jefferson, but I said Thomas Edison. Just said the wrong name, you know? Stupid."

"Then what happened?"

"She sits behind me. She said 'lightbulb' like that cartoon." He looks around for confirmation. Nobody knows the reference, so Jackson adds, "You know, with the Minions?"

"Gru!" Delaney says. "My kids love that movie."

Grant makes a note. "So, she said 'lightbulb,' and that made you mad." He waits, pen poised.

"Well, not at first, but she just kept on, you know? And I was like... fuck."

"Jackson!" I'm shocked to hear him use that word. I feel like I don't know anything about my son.

"Sorry, but she just wouldn't stop."

"So that's when you drew this?" Delaney leans forward, holding the drawing out for us to see.

"May I?" Chase asks. When Delaney nods, he takes the picture and studies it. "You did this?" There's a hint of pride in his voice.

Jackson nods. "I didn't mean it like I wanted to do anything to her. She's just always shooting shit at everybody like she's something more than she is."

"So Heather's the gun. The bullet is her words." Chase immediately grasps what Jackson tried to explain to me while we were in the kitchen.

"Yes." My son nods vehemently, his long hair swaying. "It was meant to be kinda funny—like, a joke. Well, funny, anyway."

"Tell me, son," Grant asks, all business, "where did you see a gun so close you could draw it like this?"

Jackson shrugs and looks to his father.

"I've taken him to the range a few times. You can rent almost anything." Chase steps forward, returning the drawing to Grant.

I feel blindsided but keep my mouth shut. *When did he take him to the shooting range?* Then again, this could just be Chase offering an easy explanation. I recognize that he doesn't say we have a safe full of guns in the basement.

Officer Grant holds the reproduction out to me, and I shake my head, refusing to take it as if it is not just a drawing but a real gun.

"*Call of Duty* is pretty accurate," Jackson adds.

The men sit for another beat, studying my son until Grant finally glances as his partner and nods. "Well, that pretty much lines up with what she told us." He places the drawing into its sleeve. The officers rise, bringing the interview to a close.

"How is she?" Jackson asks quietly.

The four of us look at him, hearing the concern in his voice, and my heart melts a little. Maybe he *is* a good kid.

"She's going to be all right. Her mother's not happy, but I think we can put this to rest."

"Great." Chase walks with the policemen toward the door.

As Chase closes the door behind the officers, I turn to Jackson. "That doesn't make it okay that you hit her. You understand me?" I am relieved that they aren't pressing charges but disturbed that we've given him an excuse. Words don't give him the right to hit. It doesn't make it okay just because she was in the wrong too.

"Yes, ma'am."

Chase returns to the living room, plops on the couch next to Jackson, and turns on the TV.

I should be happy we've won, but my stomach churns as he flips through channels. "So, what's next?"

Chase doesn't bother looking up at me. "What do you mean? It's over. He gets a couple of days off school. That's all."

They just sit there, watching TV like it's any other night, and my mind spins toward a future where Jackson becomes his father in some other woman's life. The small moment in the kitchen when I felt like I still knew him has been blown apart.

I leave them sitting together of the sofa to finish cleaning. I want to scream. *What the hell is wrong with Chase? How can he think this is over? It's just the beginning.*

# Chapter 14

I schedule an appointment on Thursday for Jackson to see his pediatrician. It's an effort to get him motivated and out of the house, but as we settle in to wait our turn, Jackson looks entirely out of place among the infants and toddlers. He ignores me, scrolling through YouTube videos on his phone, laughing under his breath.

"I don't understand what you think you're going to gain by doing this," Chase said when I told him I scheduled the appointment.

"I just want it on his record that he doesn't remember the incident. Maybe Dr. Philpott can explain that."

"What difference does it make? He's going back to school on Monday." He filled his travel mug and leaned against the sink.

"I know. I'll just feel better."

"Whatever." He arched then righted himself. "I gotta go. I'll be late tonight."

"Oh, why?"

"It's Birdie. I need to run through some accounting stuff with her."

"What happened to Bridget?"

"Nothing. It's Bridget I'm talking about. Everybody calls her Birdie." He leaned over and kissed my head.

"What accounting stuff? It's not like she's new." I smiled up at him, softening the judgment. *Birdie.* What a ridiculous thing to call a grown woman.

"No, she's taking over payroll. It's gonna be a pain in the ass to transition."

I frown. Chase has always done the payroll himself. It's been a point of pride. "I pay my men," he used to say.

"You must really trust her."

"She's all right. Let me know what the pediatrician says."

I stood at the front door for a long minute after he left, feeling uneasy.

In the waiting room, his excuse for staying late nags my brain. It sounds wrong, like a lie. Chase has cheated before. With Lara, the woman he was seeing when I was pregnant with Jackson. When I had confronted him, he didn't deny it, simply motioned toward my enormous stomach with his eyes wide. He was so casual, dropping that information.

*Is it cheating if he tells me where he's going to be?* The way he did with Lara. He'd say he had "business to take care of," and we both knew what he meant. After all, I was pregnant. *What else could he do?*

"Jackson Reddick?"

I jump, pulled from my reverie, feeling all sorts of wrong. I nudge Jackson so he gets up to join me. We make our way to the door where the nurse waits. Jackson towers over us, and she and I share amused looks.

"You're getting so tall, Jackson."

"Yes, ma'am."

I appreciate him using his manners and smiling at the nurse. After she shows us to our room, Jackson slouches, his hair falling forward, and the YouTube stream starts again. Between Chase's potential cheating and Jackson's detached attitude, my mind can't find rest.

Dr. Philpott knocks. Jackson removes his earbuds and slides them into his pocket.

"What brings you in?" Dr. Philpott asks after our greeting.

"Jackson had a blackout the other day. We'd like to figure out what caused it."

"Did you faint?" Dr. Philpott asks Jackson directly, and I appreciate that I don't have to try to explain.

"No."

"Would you like to tell me what happened?"

Jackson glances at me, and I realize that he is angry. He doesn't want to be here, talking to his pediatrician.

"I got in a fight and don't remember it."

Dr. Philpott asks a series of questions about if such a thing has ever happened before, when the blackouts occurred, the duration, and what he remembers from before and after. "How often has it happened?"

"I don't know. Three or four times."

"Well, let's take some blood and rule out a physiological cause. I don't think it's anything to worry about. You say it has only happened during times of extreme stress?"

"I guess."

"It's not uncommon for people to have memory lapses with stress. But let's just rule everything else out, okay?" Jackson nods, but I am unsatisfied. Dr. Philpott is not taking this as seriously as I think he should. There is something wrong with my son, and I want it fixed before he hurts anybody else.

The nurse comes back after the doctor has left and gives me paperwork for the lab. Jackson and I make our way across town to the facility to sit for another round of waiting before his blood is drawn.

THE AFTERNOON STRETCHES on into a lonely night. My senses are jagged and on edge, and it takes all my focus to finish preparing dinner. I feel like my soul is ready to burst through my skin. Chase's late-night "work" with Birdie is a sure sign that the honeymoon period is over. The fairy-tale quality of our life after I first came back has lifted, and the dread returns. It's only a matter of time before I set him off again. The next beatdown will be worse, maybe even enough to kill me. But I don't know how to get away if he has the police on his side.

Jackson comes down to eat, barely sitting to inhale his food before going back to his room. We've not spoken ten words since leaving the doctor's office. No matter how hard I've pressed, he has only offered monosyllabic responses. The flash of anger I had seen in his eyes leaves little doubt that he is punishing me. At nine, I give up waiting on him to come back down or Chase to come home and go to bed. I don't notice when Chase comes in, but at some point in the middle of the night, I turn over and feel him in the bed beside me.

# Chapter 15

On Friday, Mr. Underhill calls to offer me the position in the library at Eastside, but my temporary elation is eclipsed when Dr. Philpott calls with the results of Jackson's bloodwork. He didn't find a direct cause for Jackson's blacking out, but he does believe there may be a psychogenic cause, not unheard of in teens during times of stress. He is willing to write a letter to that effect to place in Jackson's academic file.

When his letter arrives in my email, I sit down and fill out the appeals paperwork even though Jackson is already cleared to return to school. I want my findings on record. My mind spins and rolls in on itself, worrying over how I will tell Chase that I got the job, even though he didn't want me to. Jackson is still mad at me, staying upstairs, the heavy throb of his music reverberating through the ceiling.

AFTER I DROP JACKSON off at the high school on Monday, I rush through traffic to get to Eastside. I never managed to tell Chase that I was taking the job. Not that he asked. Last Friday, he and Jackson returned home flushed and in good spirits after their first class at the Krav Maga studio. The weekend was filled with them wrestling around the living room, shooting baskets in the driveway, or watching MMA on TV. I folded laundry, cooked, and stayed out of the way.

I was invisible.

I feel about half-sick with my deceit, clinging to my cell phone. I should call Chase—make sure this is okay. Or just go home. I walk to the entrance to Eastside Elementary, determined to tell Mr. Underhill that I cannot take the job. I hold the door for kids before I get a break in the flow and can enter. Inside, Mr. Underhill makes a point to greet every single student, giving them high fives or offering fist bumps.

My stomach flips when he turns his attention on me. "Ms. Stone." The smile on his face transfers to his voice. "I'm so glad you are here."

"Oh, me too." The creep of a blush rises up my neck, and I look away from him. *What in the world is wrong with me?*

"Give me a few minutes, and we'll talk contract." He motions toward the lady behind the glass shield. "Sharon, can you take Ms. Stone to the library so she can get the lay of the land?"

Sharon smiles and opens the door, taking me through the office, introducing me to the administrative team.

"Delilah!" Carmen looks up at me from her desk and comes to the door. "So you're taking the job?" My softhearted friend is put together, professional. I cock an eyebrow at her.

"I think so." I smile, feeling Sharon standing beside me, waiting.

"Well, I'll come down and check on you when I finish here. Busy, busy, you know." She reaches out and touches my arm.

"Great. Uh, Sharon's gonna show me around." I feel so far out of my comfort zone, like I don't belong in Carmen's office world. She looks so different here—mature and formidable.

"Great." She smiles, and there my friend is again.

Sharon leads me through the school. We pause along the way as she points out or introduces everybody we meet. I am completely overwhelmed. Names slip past my ears, but I smile and nod, feeling ridiculous.

Jackson was a student at Eastside, so the library is not foreign to me. When he was here, I volunteered to work with students on their reading skills, sitting with them as they learned their spelling words.

*I could tell Chase I'm just volunteering again.* He wouldn't mind that. It's just the job that bothers him.

We stop in front of the main desk. "Evelyn, I have Ms. Stone here. She's gonna be filling in during your maternity leave."

"Oh, super." Evelyn sets the glazed donut aside and stands from the desk, her belly burgeoning as she rights herself. She extends her hand. "I'm so glad you're here."

"Me too."

She looks at me, one eyebrow rising. "I know you."

"I wondered if you would remember me. I'm Delilah."

Evelyn smiles brightly. "That's right! I'm trying to remember your son's name."

"Jackson," I offer, remembering the sweet boy he used to be. Our reunion is interrupted by the bell sending the kids to their classes. Sharon excuses herself, and after the second bell sounds, her voice comes over the intercom with morning announcements. After Evelyn asks about Jackson, and I ask what she is having—a girl—she returns to her donut, and I tuck my purse under the desk.

*It's okay. This is going to be okay.* I let Evelyn walk me through the stacks before I set about the task of putting returned books away. She logs them into the system, and I do the busywork of stooping and reaching. I'm finishing the cart when my phone vibrates. Dread fills me as I pull it from my pocket.

*What are you doing?*

I knew I would have to tell him. *I'm at Jackson's old school. Helping in the library.*

I wait. Three dots appear. After a minute, the dots disappear. My stomach flops. His silence is ominous, but I slide the phone into my pocket and finish shelving the rest of the books. Long minutes pass before my phone vibrates again.

*So you took the job?*

*Not yet.* It's true. Nick Underhill hasn't come to talk contracts yet, so I may just be helping today. I text again before Chase can respond. *I'd like to, though.*

He doesn't respond. No dots even appear.

I go with Evelyn to work the cafeteria through lunch, and Mr. Underhill asks me to meet him in his office when I am done.

Chase is going to be mad. Chase is already mad.

I STEEL MYSELF BEFORE tapping my knuckle on Mr. Underhill's door. The door tilts open, revealing him at his desk.

He looks up, a smile dimpling his cheeks. "How's it going? You haven't changed your mind, have you?"

"No. Not unless you have. It feels like old times."

"So, you know Evelyn?"

"Yeah, we go way back." I laugh, my confidence recovering. *I am strong. I am independent.*

"Come in." He stands, motioning to one of two chairs on the other side of the desk. I settle in and feel a moment of déjà vu. It occurs to me that Dr. Tate indicated a seat in the same way. Maybe it's part of some secret principal training they must go through.

"How's your son doing?"

My mouth goes dry. "Excuse me?"

"He was sick?" His brows draw together then relax.

"Oh." A faint blush warms cheeks as I remember my white lie. *Is this a test?* I wonder if all the principals get together after work to discuss the troubled cases from the day. "Well, he wasn't really *sick.* Just a bad day I guess."

"Oh. Well, that's good—not that he had a bad day, but that he wasn't sick."

I smile and nod.

He opens the folder on his desk, and I catch the scent of him as he offers me the contract in his hand. He smells like sun and outdoors—like a forest. I force myself not to draw a long breath and bring attention to my noticing.

"I didn't know when we met last week that you went to college with our assistant principal."

"Yeah. We were roommates."

"That's what she said. I bet you have some stories." He chuckles, rising from his chair and coming around to sit next to me.

"None that I'll share," I say, and we both laugh as if I have stories that would make Carmen look bad. The truth is we were boring in college, which is why that one night at the bar sticks out in my memory. That night of mischief, of mayhem, that one-night stand that derailed my life.

"Carmen is how I ended up working with Cheryl Buxton," I say.

"How's that?"

"Carmen is Cheryl's niece."

"Really?"

I nod. "Maybe I shouldn't have shared that." *Why would Carmen keep that a secret? I'll have to apologize.*

"I won't tell." He smiles, turning his attention to the contract.

"Carmen has always been private," I say, trying to backpedal, to rescind my breach of Carmen's confidence.

"Yes, she is that." He has a look in his eyes that suggests admiration or possibly interest. It makes me blush even though his attraction is clearly for Carmen and not me.

He clears his throat. "So, let's talk contract."

# Chapter 16

Chase doesn't come home after work.

I text and call, but he doesn't answer.

He's pissed.

CHASE IS ABOVE ME, his legs pressing my thighs apart, his arms rigid, holding his body up. His face lowers, his eyes half-lidded, and his lips press against mine. I can't breathe and try to turn my face away enough to clear my nose.

I can taste the bourbon on his tongue, and my stomach knots and recoils. I force my body to still, to stop straining against him. It will be easier if I don't fight.

"I called you," I whisper when he lifts his face from mine. He puts his hand over my mouth and presses me into the bed.

"Husssh, Delilah." He is very drunk. Slurring drunk. His hand fumbles off my face, and he rises onto his knees, ripping the blankets between us away. He pushes the hem of my gown above my chest, covering part of my face, and yanks at my underwear.

"Job," he mumbles. "You fucking want a job? I'll put you to work."

"Chase." I brush my hand through his hair, understanding that somehow, me taking a job *hurts* him. Me wanting a job feels like a betrayal.

He bats my touch away, and his hand lands around my neck. Panicking, I strain against him, but he presses me harder into the bed, and the tips of his fingers tighten. At the same time, he rocks down, and his penis rips into my flesh. I jerk, trying to shift away, but his face drops low, and his body tightens all around me, pinning me.

As he forces himself deeper, his hand comes free of my neck, and I can breathe. "You're hurting me," I whisper, afraid he will hear, afraid I will make him angrier. "Chase."

His face is beside my ear as he answers my plea with low, guttural noises, more beast than man. The stink of the bourbon washes over my face as he growls.

I turn away, seeking air. "Chase. Please." My eyes land on the black outside the window, the crescent of the moon hanging in the pane.

He thrusts.

I breathe. I am beyond the window and out in the cool night air. I am on the moon. I am far, far away. He thrusts. I am in the bed. His words are incoherent in my ear. I close my eyes, thinking of anything else—the way Mr. Underhill seemed curious about Carmen, the feel of the books in my hands, the satisfaction of putting them on the shelves.

Chase thrusts. He will sleep when he is done. He will sleep, and he won't remember in the morning.

He grunts, releases, then collapses on me. I do not dare to move until he's snoring. With stealthy movements, I extract myself from beneath him, rolling him onto the mattress. He snorts and pulls the blankets up.

Once I am alone in the bathroom, hot tears sting my eyes, which only makes me furious. *I* came back to him. Of course this was going to happen. I was stupid to think I could get a job and there would not be consequences. There are always consequences. I should have waited until I was free of him.

I let the shower run and collect clothes from the closet. I throw my nightgown into the hamper as if it was the one who assaulted me.

I had a plan.

Then I came home and fell right back into the groove of our life. I'm not even angry at him. It's not like I *believed* he would really change.

I'm angry at me. The minutes click past, and the water runs down my body.

It is the darkest hour of the night when I dry myself off and get dressed. I squat in the closet, my hair still wrapped in a towel, and retrieve my secret phone from the bottom drawer.

# Chapter 17

I go through a pot of coffee early Tuesday morning before going up to wake Chase and Jackson. I am still in the jeans and sweatshirt I threw on in the middle of the night. I'll have to change to go to the school, but I'll wait till Chase is gone.

"I've got coffee," I whisper, setting a steaming cup on his bedside table.

"Mm-hmm." He doesn't crack his eyelids, but he rolls over onto his back and slides his tongue over his lips.

"Water?"

He nods, and I leave the room to fetch the water and Tylenol.

AFTER CHASE IS GONE, I change for work and drive Jackson to the high school. He is quiet, staring out the window. He must feel me looking at him because he turns, catches my eye in the mirror, then removes his earbud. "What?"

I almost laugh. "Nothing. I didn't say anything."

He nods, and we both return to our separate windows.

"You okay?" he asks when we stop at a light.

"What? Yeah, I'm fine. Why?"

He gives an elaborate shrug, and the light turns, drawing my attention.

When I glance at him again, he has replaced his earbuds, but I keep hearing his question repeating in my mind. *Did he hear something last night?* I'm confident that I didn't make any sounds that would have traveled through the house.

"Mom?" His hand reaches up and rests on my shoulder for a split second. "I'm going to talk to Heather today. Tell her I am sorry, like, really. I don't want to be *that* guy."

Tears spring to my eyes. "I'm so glad. It's the right thing to do. An apology can go a long way."

"I'll never hit a girl again. I won't."

"I hope not." We catch eyes in the rearview mirror, and he looks older than fourteen, filled with regret and resolve. "It is big for you to do that."

He nods and turns to look out the window. His jaw flexes as if he has more words that he needs to say, but they are stuck.

We reach the drop-off, and I turn to offer him my most reassuring smile, grateful that the flood of tears had time to subside. He gathers his pack and slides out of the back seat. He slams the door and walks toward the school, his shoulders hunched forward and his head down. The hollow pit in my soul grows and frays. His words mean so much. I hope he never forgets them.

THE ELEMENTARY SCHOOL is on full bustle when I park in the staff lot, so I avoid the front entrance and go in through the cafeteria. My son's sudden attitude shift has me distracted and second-guessing myself. *What brought that up?* He said he didn't want to be "that guy." *Did he see something?* My stomach plummets. Chase had my neck last night. He may have left marks. I sneak into the teachers' lounge and pass through to the bathroom to check. The fluorescent light buzzes, and I lean over the sink, studying my neck for bruises.

Nothing. I step back and push my hands through my hair. I look fine, just tired. Maybe he heard me up this morning earlier than normal. Maybe it wasn't about me at all. Maybe it was just that he finally wanted to tell me about Heather. That must have been it. Relieved, I leave the bathroom.

The flood of kids moving down the hall sweeps me along until I reach the library, which is still locked. I check my watch, surprised that I'm the first one here. Evelyn gave me a key yesterday, and I fumble for it in my bag. It feels like entering a church or some other reverent place, with the fluorescents off and the stacks silent. I flip on the lights and make my way around the counter to boot up the computer.

Within minutes, the room wakes, and the first student of the day comes in. She's tall and skinny, probably fifth grade. Her hair is pulled up into a fuzzy ball on top of her head. After greeting her, she hands over a book to return.

"Did you like it?" I ask the way Evelyn would if she were here.

"Yeah. It was okay." The girl makes her way to the stacks and returns with another book by the same author.

"You liked the author at least."

She nods, and we stand for a second while the computer finishes logging on. I check the book out, and she leaves me alone in my quiet place. Since Evelyn hasn't come in yet, I pull the rack of books to be put away and start the process of sorting them.

"How's it going?" Carmen asks from the doorway.

"Good. Where's Evelyn?"

"She's gone into labor. This is all yours." She spreads her arms to encompass the library, and my heart swells.

*Mine.* It's only my second day, and they already trust me to handle this while Evelyn is gone. Another person might take this opportunity for granted, but to me, on this day, it feels like a gift.

# Chapter 18

That afternoon, Jackson stays after school to practice for basketball tryouts, so I drive to the old part of town where Chase's mother lives in Waterstone Manor. It's a nice facility, and Geneva seems happy here. I try to visit at least once every week. Chase comes for holidays and birthdays.

It is just after three o'clock when I park my car and head through the parking lot. I pause to speak to the old woman standing near the entrance. "Hi, Mrs. Tillman."

"Have you seen my Harry?"

"Not today, I haven't. Is he coming to visit?" I've been having some version of this conversation with Mrs. Tillman for almost a year. Mr. Tillman passed away, but she still expects him to visit.

"He was supposed to be here by now. He's taking me to the picture show." She wrings her hands together, fretting that he is late.

"It will be nice to see him." She won't remember speaking with me, so it's better not to try to explain that Harry passed away and won't be coming today. She lives her entire life in frantic anticipation of his arrival.

"Yes. It will be so nice." She sighs.

After signing in, I leave her for the elevators. Geneva's suite is on the second floor, but she is not in her room. I find her in the lounge with several other women, watching television.

"Hey, Miss Geneva." I slide into the seat next her. "What are you watching?"

It's one of those CSI shows, and she takes my hand and gives me the quick rundown of the case. I sit with her until the program ends, knowing her well enough not to interrupt.

"That was interesting," I offer when the riddle is solved, the bad guy discovered and brought to justice.

She makes a dismissive face, positions her four-pronged cane, then hoists herself up from the chair. She is independent and does not appreciate being coddled, so I ignore the urge to help. It was a broken hip that landed her in here. She still isn't steady but hasn't lost her balance in months. It was supposed to be temporary, just until she could get back on her feet, but she doesn't want to go home to an empty house, and at least here, there are people.

Once she is on her feet, she asks, "How is everybody?"

"Everybody is good. I took a job."

"You did? What are you doing?"

I slow my pace to hers, and we amble over to the elevators. "I'm working in the library at the elementary school. Their regular librarian is out on maternity."

She furrows her brow, bunching the papery skin, and straightens. "I don't understand why you don't work at the company. That's where you should be. It doesn't make any sense."

Geneva was forty when Chase was born, a sole child to a woman who had thought she was barren. She doted on her son but never let that keep her from a day job. "You should be his helpmate. I loved working with my Vern. We were a team."

"I know." I smile, my affection toward Geneva tinged with annoyance. She thinks that it is my decision not to be there. I can't even begin to explain how much Chase doesn't want me in the office.

My failure to join the team is not the only thing Geneva has misunderstood about me and her son. The company was always meant to be Chase's, but when Vern was ready to hand it down, Geneva was worried that we weren't married. Jackson was two then. She was afraid of us breaking up and me taking her grandson somewhere out of reach. They had spoken with Chase, urged him to marry me, to solidify his family, but he had told them what he told me—he didn't believe in marriage. He was furious when they put together a contract and forced him to agree to it. Then they marched us down to the courthouse for a five-minute civil ceremony before they would give him charge of the company. Geneva insisted that both of our names be listed as owners because that was how she and Vern had done it.

Chase had acquiesced, but I paid the price. He hated the stipulation that I could only be removed once Jackson, and any other progeny—Geneva loved Jackson and wanted us to have ten more just like him—reached the age of majority, at which time ownership could be transferred to our kids. Chase felt betrayed and believed that I had plotted against him. He made it clear that I was not wanted, so I never had a hand in the running of the business. I wouldn't dare, except to sign for loans and to arrange for the food at his annual company party.

With her meddling, Geneva intended to give me a sense of security, but she put me in danger instead. It's Chase's company, and we both know it.

"Chase is so good at running things," I say. "He doesn't want me poking around."

We make our way through the lobby and sit in the garden as we do every week. I confide in her about Jackson's fight, leaving out the detail of Heather's gender. "I just worry about him. Sometimes, he seems so angry."

"Boys do. Phew. Chase was just the same, always itching for a fight."

"Yeah, I reckon so. They do grow up, though," I say as if Chase has stopped itching for a fight. "Was Vern like that? Did he have a temper?" I can't look at her as I ask this, afraid that the truth will shine in my eyes.

"Pfft."

*What does* that *mean?* But Geneva doesn't give any other clues.

"Jackson is just fine. Boys fight."

I nod. It is exactly what Chase said. "I'm sure you're right."

An old man steps into the garden and shambles around the path. He stops when he reaches us, and I can't help but smirk as he speaks to Geneva. "We're playing whist up in the dining hall in half an hour. I need a partner. You in?"

Geneva agrees, then the old man turns and shuffles back into the building.

"How is Mr. Robbins?" I ask, feeling sly. They've flirted a bit over the past year.

"Well, you saw him." She is dismissive.

"I thought you kinda liked him."

"Oh, phooey. What good would that do me? I already had one man. I don't need any more of that." She squeezes my arm, and we smile and nod. That's Geneva—a truth teller if ever there was one.

A little later, after I promise to bring Jackson with me next time, we make our way inside. I leave Geneva at the elevators with a hug. On my way out, I pass Mrs. Tillman again, still waiting for her husband.

# Chapter 19

The weeks tick by. I change out the Welcome Back display at the library entrance to Here Comes Fall. Evelyn was detailed about when I should make changes and even left me lists of the books that I should display each month. I try to fill her shoes. I talk to every student who comes in and am friendly and polite. Using the sticker system Evelyn set up, I help them find the right color dot to discover books that might get them interested in reading.

Between students, there's plenty of spare time to think about Chase and my escape plan—the plan I let fall through the cracks as if I liked his beatdowns. He is late coming home almost every night, and he has gone to work on every Saturday since I took the job. I know he's punishing me. The tension is ramping up. The explosion is coming. And soon. I have to take the next step, but it feels like the plan is sketchy, far-fetched.

After helping in the cafeteria through lunch, I come back to the library and sit down at Evelyn's desk. The computer screen is black in front of me, sleeping. I stare at it, hesitating. The faint reflection of my face looks back until I touch the space bar, and the screen glows. When I open the web browser, which I haven't dared to do until today, a tab opens. I type *Michael Dietz* in the search bar then narrow it by adding *Aldrich GA*.

Several stories appear. The first headline, from the *Aldrich Herald*, says "Local Man Murdered."

The snippet below reads, *Aldrich was shocked on Friday evening when a Drake man was discovered bludgeoned to death in the back bed-*

*room of a known party house. Police are actively investigating and are confident they will have the perpetrator in custody soon. Detective Young...*

I click the snippet to get the rest of the story, but the archives are locked unless I pay for access. I skip to the next story, "Police Have a Lead!"

*Detective Young says they are getting close to an arrest in the brutal slaying of 22-year-old Michael Dietz. Last Friday, Dietz attended a party at a home on Second Street and was discovered in a back bedroom around 10 p.m. Detective...*

I click out of the newspaper sites and return to my Bing search. Results flood in, and I scroll through them, gleaning information and wishing I paid more attention when it happened. It was a big deal in Aldrich, where the university is, and in Drake, where Michael Dietz grew up. Where Chase grew up. Where I went to high school after my mom died.

The murder took place in a house directly across the street from the Warehouse, which was the last bar my roommates and I went to that fateful night. That bar was the last place I ever went before Chase derailed my life.

WE WALKED THE EIGHT blocks to the square, four girls at the end of our last year of college, on the edge of taking the world by storm. It was already dark, and I was wishing that I hadn't agreed to join them. Bars populated the low-rent section on and off the town square: Stan's, Mother's, the Downtowner, the Warehouse, and Steel to name a few. The buildings were old, the wiring faulty, and the floors just a step below sticky. We stopped at the Downtowner, which was crowded and loud. It was nearly impossible to get drinks. It seemed everybody was out to celebrate the end of the year.

Our tongues syrupy from the first drink of the night, we moved through the crowd at the Downtowner and back onto the street. Mother's was overflowing as well, so we decided to keep going. The Warehouse was less crowded, so we had made our way inside. We ordered drinks that suggested we were more adventuresome than we were—Sex on the Beach, Between the Sheets, and a round of Buttery Nipples, with tequila shots in between.

Sharla peeled free of our group first, joining another teacher in the making. The rest of us stood watching a pair of boys shooting pool. We tried to talk above the chaos but finally settled for bouncing hips to the rhythm of a beat so distorted it couldn't quite qualify as music.

I didn't belong in the bar. It was full of strangers I didn't want to know. I looked at the door, wishing I was back at the dorm with *The X-Files*. Then the door swung open, and Chase Reddick swept into the bar. His shoulder-length blond hair swayed as he beelined for the bathroom.

My stomach plummeted, and I looked for the nearest exit. Chase Reddick still caused my heart to jump in my chest, and we hadn't even been in the same room since the end of my first semester. My eyes moved away then bounced back to the bathroom door, time and again, until he emerged, his hair slicked back by wet hands. He looked wild and was wiping at a wet spot on his T-shirt with a paper towel. Chase was a train wreck, and I couldn't look away. A glutton for punishment, I couldn't help but wonder what girl he was meeting there.

But he didn't join a girl. He went to the bar, ordered, and waited. His hand tapped his thigh to a rhythm of its own, out of sync to the music, his eyes darting through the crowd. The bar was his scene, and when his drink slid across the smooth gloss of the wood, he rapped his knuckles against the surface, two solid knocks. He was centered and in control again.

My mouth went dry, and I drew my lower lip between my teeth to wet it, still watching. He was familiar to me, and though our affair had been short-lived, my body remembered what it was like to be with him.

As he drew the beer to his lips, my eyes traveled the length of him. He'd grown thicker, more solid, and his once-gangly limbs had filled out into fully mature muscles. The wet spot on the front of his shirt clung to him.

Freshman year, I was infatuated the moment he set his sights on me. I'd had a quiet crush on him my senior year of high school, but he hadn't known I existed. When he approached me in college, I fell into him like water into a glass. I was devastated when he dropped me flat. Shame flamed on my cheeks, remembering how I'd lingered in places where I thought he might be for months after he stopped calling.

The body beneath the wet T-shirt stilled. My eyes swept to his face, and I nearly choked when I saw that he was looking at me. A bemused half smile titled his lips as if he hadn't broken my heart. I faltered and dropped my face, blushing. Turning away, I nudged Carmen's shoulder as if she just said something hilarious. With the flood of the alcohol rushing through my veins, I mustered the courage to glance back at the bar. But he was walking across the room, directly toward us. An eyebrow was cocked high on his forehead, his hair moving with each step. I tried to look away but was trapped in his tractor beam, held captive.

Surely, he wasn't coming for me—not after all this time. After he'd made it clear that I was not the type of girl he wanted. If he came for Carmen, I would die.

But when Chase Reddick approached, it was as if Carmen wasn't even there. "If it isn't Delilah Stone."

"Oh my God. You *do* remember my name." I tried to sound mocking or coy, as if all those years when I had been invisible to him hadn't hurt.

"Of course." His lips spread wide, and my resolve liquified. I barely paid any mind to the fact that the pale blue of his eyes was just a rim around his enlarged pupils, and a high flush rode on his cheekbones. His voice melted me. "I've been here all night, watching you, thinking about how much I've missed you. Why did we stop seeing each other? Can I buy you a drink?"

And then I was lost.

# Chapter 20

We were probably at the bar when that poor kid was dying.

I tap on the keyboard and bring up the next story. A man was arrested, charged, and convicted of Dietz's murder before the next semester was even in session. Dabney Holt, the boy who *discovered* the body, was the only real suspect. He had no defense and is fourteen years into a twenty-year sentence at Dorrell, the state penitentiary. But I know there's another suspect. I wonder why I'm the only one who thinks Chase is capable of it.

*This is crazy.* My fingers trace my eyebrow, and I click from one story to the next until I reach a blog called *Just InJustice*, which highlights wrongful convictions. Dabney Holt is featured. The photograph of Holt shows him in prison orange with a shaved head and trimmed beard.

*Dabney Holt is a victim of police rush to justice. He was accused and convicted of murdering a known drug dealer in a party house. Holt was unable to mount an adequate defense, as the prosecution pushed to set a speedy trial. Additionally, the court-appointed counsel had conflicting interests, as his wife was on the board of trustees for the local university, and he admitted to* Just InJustice *that there was great pressure to close the case before the fall semester. The town convicted one of its own of a crime he did not commit to line its own coffers.*

*The evidence against Holt was circumstantial at best. Yes, Holt was present the night in question. Yes, he had been in the room where Michael Dietz was discovered, as were any number of partygoers. The room produced eighteen different DNA profiles, but only seventeen were matched.*

*Why did the police not pursue all the leads? We at* Just InJustice *believe that the eighteenth profile, the one that was never matched, belongs to the person responsible for this horrendous crime. Where was DNA sample 18 found? On the blood-soaked T-shirt the victim was wearing, friends. The only foreign sample on the victim's body, and the police did not even follow it up. Had they discovered the identity of DNA sample 18, would they have uncovered the missing murder weapon as well?*

*The sheer fact that Dabney's DNA profile was not among the three samples discovered on the body was not even presented at the trial. One of the profiles belonged to the victim, one to a girl Dietz had visited prior, who was questioned by police, and the third belonged to DNA profile 18, which was never brought up in front of a jury. Nor was the fact that DNA profile 18 was unaccounted for presented to the jury.*

*Dabney Holt was charged because he was poor, because he discovered the body, and because, while in the throes of an LSD experience, he thought what he discovered wasn't real. He didn't raise the alarm in his altered state. He returned to the party and began suggesting that somebody else should check on Michael Dietz.*

*Is Holt guilty of poor judgment? Yes. But he is not guilty of the crime he is currently serving time for in Dorrell Penitentiary.*

Just InJustice *tracked down an Aldrich police officer who was close to the case. He agreed to speak with us anonymously. To answer our questions regarding the speed of the arrest and lackluster policework, he said, "The city officials were worried that college enrollment would drop and hurt the town's financials if the murder was left unsolved. They pushed us to make an arrest, and Holt was our only arrest-worthy suspect at the time."*

*There you have it. Dabney Holt was a patsy, and the prosecution knew it.* Just InJustice *is working to right this wrong. Sign our petition to force the courts to review the Holt case.*

Beneath the article is a button to sign the petition. I let the cursor sit, hovering over the button while my head spins.

*What am I doing?* I close the browser and consider my next move. What they need is a sample of Chase's DNA to see if he matches the missing eighteenth sample. That should be easy enough to accomplish. But I would have to find the Aldrich detective who spoke with *Just InJustice* and hope he still has an interest in the case.

Then I remember the familiarity between Chase and the two officers that came to our home. The police are not an option. If I contact *Just InJustice* directly and help them start digging, they might ask for my name. They could show up at our house and start harassing Chase, and I cannot imagine putting Jackson through that. Besides, Chase would find out that I put them on his trail. No one else would.

# Chapter 21

Chase continues to avoid me. He hasn't touched me since the night he came home so late, after I took the job.

*Does he remember what he did?* That could be why he's keeping his distance. Maybe he's waiting for me to suggest counseling again so he can explode and release the anger I see veiled behind his eyes. I won't. I know he is never going to therapy with me. That was just me hoping I wouldn't have to follow through with the plan. I was giving him one last chance.

One more last chance.

I drop a chicken breast into the egg wash then toss it in breadcrumbs. Chase and Jackson are at Krav Maga, so they'll be hungry when they get home. It's important that Chase doesn't feel like the house is suffering because of my job. If I keep on top of everything, maybe he'll let me keep working even after Evelyn comes back from maternity leave.

My mind roils, contemplating my plan. If I cannot go to the police or the media myself, I must meet with Dabney Holt. I'm clueless as to whether he knows Chase or will remember him being at the party that night. But if I visit, I could subtly encourage him to put Chase on somebody's radar. Surely, he has a lawyer—for what little good that did him. But he has *Just InJustice*.

My phone vibrates, and Carmen's face lights the screen. I answer using the knuckle of my pinkie.

"You alone?" Carmen asks in a pinched tone.

"Yeah."

"Take me off speaker." She always knows, says she hears it in the ambient noise.

"Okay, just a sec." I wash my hands and return to pick up the phone. "What's wrong?"

"Who is Michael Dietz?"

I stammer, unable to form a coherent response.

"Are you having an affair? Did you meet somebody?"

"God, no. He was a kid I knew from high school. What made you ask about him?"

"I guess I should have mentioned that the school tracks keystrokes."

My face is on fire, and my stomach sours. "Am I in trouble?"

"If he's a porn star, yeah, probably." She doesn't sound like the vice principal. She sounds like my friend, and my stomach settles.

"He's dead. He's not a porn star."

"Why are you looking him up?"

"He went to our high school. He died the year we graduated from college." I glance through the living room to where I can see the front door.

"So? Why are you looking him up?" she asks, her voice dropping into conspiratorial tones. I can hear her typing.

"I can't talk about it." I step out the back door and stand on the deck overlooking the backyard. Chase and Jackson could be home any minute, and I don't want him to overhear anything.

"Shit. I remember this. This was a big deal." I hear her keys clicking, and I imagine her scanning the sites I visited on the school computer.

"Yep, right before graduation."

She makes a sharp intake of breath. "Shit. That's horrible."

I wonder which article caused that reaction. "Yeah. It was. Look, I have to go. I've got to get dinner ready."

"Okay," she says, but I hear the hesitation, the need for more understanding in her voice. "Seriously, why are you looking this guy up?"

I hesitate and glance back into the house. The front door is still closed. "You remember that I said I had a plan?"

"Yeah." She sounds dubious.

"He's part of the plan."

"Fuck." Carmen has always been smart. It took me all of these years to understand what happened that night, and all it took for her to put it together was for me to mention it.

"Yeah, fuck."

We disconnect, and I slip the phone into my hip pocket and return to the kitchen. The rolling in my head that has plagued me since I found Michael's name calms. I'm not alone anymore. Carmen is in on it now, and even if I don't have the courage to take him down, she will. She'll know how to put Chase on the radar.

I lower the meat into the frying pan exactly the way Geneva taught me. It's one of Chase's favorite meals, full of starch and carbs like everything his mother cooked. I check the potatoes in the oven, gauging my time.

Maybe I could send the police an email from my burner phone and tell them about Chase without giving anything about my identity away. But I am afraid his friends would go to him, and then he would see my plan.

Does my silence for all these years make me an accomplice? The idea hits me like a bolt of lightning. *I lied to the police, didn't I?*

*Did I?*

My phone vibrates.

*Taking Jack to dinner. We'll be home later.*

I stare at my phone until the screen goes dark. I wash my hands and type back. *I'm cooking.*

*We'll eat it tomorrow. Want us to pick anything up for you? We're at Johnny's.*

I turn the chicken in the skillet. It won't take but another few minutes to finish frying. I'm still dressed from work, so I text back, *I guess I could come join you.*

The three dots appear, disappear, then come up again. *Nah, we've already ordered. We'd be done before you could get here. See you at home.*

My heart jerks and hammers. I try to convince myself it's not a rejection. *He offered to bring me something, so he's thinking of me.*

It doesn't help. Of course it's a rejection. He is still punishing me for taking the job. Johnny's is one of my favorite restaurants. He knew I would be disappointed not to be invited.

By the time the chicken is fried, I've turned the corner from disappointment to anger. I let the chicken rest before I wrap it for the fridge. My emotions bound from sorrow to rage. This is just another confirmation that he does not care about me. That alone should make it easier for me to move forward, but I haven't done anything.

I'm tempted to call Carmen back, to talk through the stuff in my head and see if she thinks the same thing I do. To see if she can figure out how take a step without crossing the line with Chase. I text, *They are going out for dinner. I can talk if you can.*

## Chapter 22

Carmen does better than calling. She comes over. We do not go inside but sit on the front porch so we will see Chase coming. Bruce is across the street, looking out his window. I wave and smile, sitting in plain sight, hoping to keep his wretched imagination in check.

"What do you think this means?" Carmen gestures as if she is holding the yearbook and Chase's damning note in front of her.

I am unable to form the words.

"You think he did this? Did he kill Michael Dietz?"

I move my head up and down slowly, refusing to look at her.

"Fuck, Delilah. Did you know?"

"No, I didn't know! I didn't even pay attention to it then. Did you? It was such a whirlwind. Do you remember? Right before graduation, and it was just crazy."

"I was questioned by the police about this," Carmen says, her tone reverent.

I nod. "Me too. Not that night but the next day, after it hit the news."

The night of the crime, Chase and I snuck out a side door and down the alley before they locked down the Warehouse.

"What did you tell them?"

"That we'd been together all night." It feels like a snake uncoiling from my mouth, and I know there is no going back.

"But he wasn't. I saw him come in." Her eyes widen.

"Me too." My scalp prickles, and I run my hands through my hair, looking down the street. Any minute now, he might pull up to find us talking, and that will be the thing that lights his fuse. I tell her what I remember from that night and about Dabney Holt.

"That's where we need to start. We need to meet with him and see if he seems guilty. If he does, we drop it. If he doesn't, we talk to the police."

I could hug her for taking the reins. Where I am overwhelmed by the sheer thought of moving forward, Carmen is bold. Fearless. But it isn't that simple.

"We can't talk to the police. They are all Chase's friends." A car drives onto our street, and my heart hammers. "You gotta go, though."

It isn't Chase. But the next one may be. I walk her down the steps, and we hug before she gets in her car and drives away. She's given me direction.

Once I'm alone in the house, I fetch my secret phone and scan Dorrell Penitentiary's website, which confirms that a drop-in visit to Dabney Holt is not an option. To get on his approved visitor list, we'll need to fill out applications, allow the prison to run background checks. Then we'll have to convince Dabney Holt that he wants to meet us. But I see no reason why Carmen or I might be denied. We aren't on probation or felons. I text the link from my secret phone to Carmen, asking her to print the application form. My stomach folds in on itself as I hit Send.

After storing the burner phone, I sit in the living room and listen for the garage door. My stomach rumbles, hunger and frustration taking their toll. I check the time. Pace from kitchen to hall and down to the bedroom. I climb the steps, peek into Jackson's room, then gather the dirty clothes from his floor and add them to the hamper.

*Where are they?*

Finally, the garage door churns.

"Man, I can't believe the way she took you down!" Jackson's excited voice echoes up the stairs.

Chase chuckles. "She's a hell of a chick."

I stop to listen, bringing my foot back up and off the first step. *A girl?* They must've met her at the Krav Maga class.

"Yeah, she's awesome."

I blink. Jackson has never shown interest in anybody before. *Oh my God! He has a crush.* I don't want to interrupt, hoping to hear more.

"Delilah?" Chase calls out, summoning me.

"How was it?" I call from the steps.

"It's good. He's a natural. Those elbows." Chase feints an elbow strike, and Jackson blocks. They look like brothers. He holds the to-go bag up to me then leaves it sitting on the coffee table.

"Yeah. Dad got taken down by a girl." Jackson laughs.

Chase cocks an eyebrow then turns into the kitchen.

"I wish I could have seen that." I reach the bottom of the stairs while Chase is in the kitchen, filling a glass with water from the dispenser on the refrigerator.

"Yeah, and Birdie, she's like five-two. She's shorter than you."

"Really? Maybe I should take Krav Maga." The name "Birdie" sits like a lead in my gut. It has to be the same woman.

Chase chuckles. "Yeah, right. That'd be something to see."

I let the inherent insult pass without contest. "Birdie? Is that Bridget?"

"Yeah. She's a badass." He brushes past me, moving into the living room.

I tilt my head, feigning curiosity. "She does Krav Maga with you?"

"Well, I wouldn't say she does it with me. She's been doing it for years." He flops onto the sofa and clicks on the television. "Does it matter?"

"No. Just trying to put faces to names." I smile and pick up the bag from the table. A fresh wave of annoyance flows through me when I look inside and see that he only brought me his leftovers. I put it in the fridge then return to the living room to make sure he has everything he needs.

Chase flips through channels, searching for MMA or boxing, barely acknowledging my presence. I stand behind his chair for a moment as the channels flit and wish I had that bat. I'd knock him over the head and leave him for dead. Finally, he settles on a boxing replay, done with me.

I breathe. "I'm heading up to bed."

He nods.

THE NIGHT MICHAEL DIETZ died, I hadn't wanted Chase to know how much I missed him, how incomplete I felt. I didn't want to get sucked into my infatuation again. I hesitated, looking to my friends for guidance, but Carmen was already strutting away, one arm thrown up over her head. She'd already seen me through Chase once. She wasn't going to do it again. Chloe arched an eyebrow and tilted her head, not knowing that he and I had history.

"I'd love to catch up," he said.

"I'd like that." I stammered, feeling the heat of the tequila in my blood.

He leaned close, and his finger traced a line down my bare arm. It was as if he was taking my panties down. I nearly melted into his touch.

"Go." Chloe gave me a forceful nudge. She had to have seen my reaction.

"Okay." As I turned to face him, I was swept away by his beauty. He always had been beautiful, but he still looked a bit of a loose cannon too. He was devilish then—and dangerous. He still was.

As he led me away to a dark corner of the bar, he talked like a whirling dervish. Asked about my classes, plans, and about my dad, who always liked him. He filled me in on his job, his family, and his life since we last spoke. The years behind us warped and folded until we are just kids again, fresh out of high school. He had been my first love. I wondered why we'd ever broken up.

"I've been here all night, watching you," he whispered again, close to my ear.

There'd been a time when I couldn't walk into a building where Chase was without immediately knowing he was there. That same sensation caused me to look up at the door that night. As if I'd felt him entering the room. He'd always been intense, but that night, he was crackling with energy, and I felt exposed next to him, like I'd left my clothes at home. My head wasn't sure that I wanted to get involved with him again, but my body leaned and melded into his torso like it was home. Everything moved too fast.

"Why now?" I asked when his face was close, his mouth touching the sensitive skin on my collarbone. His hands were too much, too hungry.

"I heard you were going places. Big places." His voice was so low and close in my ear that I could feel the heat of his breath.

"Umm, I don't—"

"I wanna go with you. I can't *lose* you."

I purred, but the irony of his words wasn't lost on me. I'd pursued him for six months, and he'd wanted nothing to do with me. I hadn't heard from him in over three years, but after graduation, I was headed to New York. And suddenly, he wanted to rejoin my life.

I should have turned and walked away then, with the shoe on the other foot. The thought crossed my mind to smile up at him and tap him on the cheek with a loving hand, saying, "Oh, Chase, that's so sweet. But I don't want you to go with me. I don't want you anymore." I imagined myself turning and walking away with a swish of my hips.

But my small, sweet vengeance was dampened with a kiss, with hands, with another drink replacing the one I finished. Under his spell, my body was liquid, and it felt so good to be the center of his attention again. We drank and danced, and soon, we were kissing in long, breathless measures. Tipsy and caught in the cyclone of Chase, I forgot my reservations entirely. That I had a plan, a future. My body was charged and on fire with his touch.

"Let's get out of here?" His voice was deep, rumbling along my neck.

I nodded and found Chloe. "I'll see you back at the quad."

It felt like daring the devil to be on his arm again. It felt like danger.

We went out the side door and down the alley, headed into the future, entwined like a single organism. Behind us, the flashing lights of a pod of police cars and an ambulance drew my attention. I strained to see and watched the paramedics loading the stretcher into the ambulance.

To this day, I can almost feel the phantom pressure from his hand on my back as I remember his words. "Don't look back there, babe. Come on. Don't look over there."

I let him turn me, hurry me down the alley and out onto Elm. A block past the alley, he darted into a yard and leaned into some bushes beside the house. He came out with a baseball bat and tapped it lightly against the trees we passed, all the way to his apartment.

# Chapter 23

If Dabney Holt admits that he killed that kid, then I'll have to find another way out. But my mind is revving and connecting dots.

Carmen took the lead and came up with a cover story for our visit. She pops in at work to show me the letter, and I scan it, impressed with the way her mind works.

*We are part the advance team for Cheryl Buxton, author. She is considering your case for a future project, and we would appreciate the opportunity to speak with you on her behalf.*

She even thought to include me as her assistant. I give her my completed application, and she folds it into the envelope with hers.

"Now we wait." She winks and leaves me alone in the library.

IT IS A RARE EVENING that Jackson does not have basketball or Krav Maga to attend, but tonight, he is up in his room. Chase is going to be late as they try to finish a project to get back on schedule. I move through the house, wiping dust from surfaces. I lift the keyboard for the computer to swipe beneath it, and the computer wakes. The screen is open to Chase's email. I pause, my eyes running down the line of emails, and in the second before I turn away, I see the name *Bird*. The email has already been read.

I move the cursor over it and click. The email opens.

*For when you are missing me – B.*

A video is attached.

I hesitate.

Steeling myself, I click and wait as the video blooms across the screen. A small woman is stretched naked on a bed. One arm is flung across her face.

"Look at me." The sound of Chase's voice sends chills down my spine.

She is young, probably in her twenties. When she looks at him, her black hair slips across her forehead, her pretty face pink with nerves or excitement. "No." She turns away again.

I sink into the chair, and my soul vacates my body as Chase's naked backside breaches the screen, walking with such confidence toward the bed. Mesmerized and horrified, I can't look away as he kneels between her legs. I let the video run, my hands drawn up over my mouth, my eyes stinging.

He makes love with her. He is tender and caressing, and she moans into him. His hand never once closes around her throat.

When the video ends, I click on the file and choose the Save As option. I save it into my folder as *System990*. It's a nothing title, something that nobody would think anything of. I close out of the email.

I leave the computer as it was before, open to Chase's email.

Suddenly, with evidence, the late nights make perfect sense. I am up the stairs, pulling my duffle from the closet. I do not have to stay. Rage racks my body, fury like I have never known.

*Who does he think he is?* After everything he has put me through. I feel sick at the thought of Chase replacing me with a younger, updated model, and my stomach twists when I realize he's already introduced Jackson to her. Are they going to steal my son? Jackson probably knows something is going on between them. That's why he asked me if I was okay the other morning. He was trying to gauge my response.

Chase's empty promises about things being different and going to therapy shatter at my feet.

*You were nothing but an alibi.* The line from his note erupts into the room as if it was spoken.

My finger travels the path of my eyebrow. If I leave now, it will be a fight. If I try to take Jackson out of this house, it will be worse.

I have to get ahead of this. Use my mind and not just react. Every fiber of me wants to make Jackson see him for what he is.

I go back to the computer and open my email account, minimizing his into the corner. I type an email to Carmen.

*Do not open this file, but keep it somewhere safe. Please. I'll explain later.* I attach the file and hit Send.

A minute later, my phone vibrates.

"What is this?" Carmen asks when I answer, and I can almost picture her brows raised in question.

"Evidence. It came through?"

"Yeah, seems to have. What is it?"

"He's having an affair," I whisper into the phone as I delete the sent email from my account and close the browser. Carmen has questions, but I'm not listening to her. "I have to go. I'll explain tomorrow."

After taking a deep breath, I go back into my bedroom and put my duffle away, tidying the room to its previous condition. Then I carry on with my dusting as though it never happened. But inside, I'm barely keeping it together. I am confused by how much the video hurt. I want to be free of Chase. If he has somebody new, I should just let him go and wish her the best of luck. I stop at Jackson's room and knock on the door.

"Come in," he calls, and I push the door open. He is bowed over his laptop on his bed.

"Hey, buddy. What do you want for dinner?"

"I don't care."

I sit down on the edge of the bed and look around his room. I didn't actually expect him to have an idea about dinner. It was just an excuse to not be alone. My heart has been skewered, and I am bleeding out into my chest.

"You doing all right? Is everything okay at school?"

"Yeah. Tate hates me, but I don't care."

"He doesn't hate you, Jackson, he just thinks you have anger issues. Do you feel like the Krav Maga is helping?" I have concerns about him taking martial arts when the problem is his tendency toward violence. Jackson is already strong—he doesn't need to be lethal. *Is it making Chase more lethal?*

"Yeah, it's a good outlet."

"So, Birdie's pretty good, huh?" My voice sounds tight, saying her name.

"Yeah."

His one-word answer grates at me. I want him to tell me about her, but he can't know much from classes. "You know she works with Daddy."

"Yeah." He doesn't seem interested.

"Did they seem like they get along well?" I'm crossing a line, but my brain is screaming, *Do you know he is cheating on me? Do you know they are fucking?*

But Jackson never looks up from his screen. "Yeah. She's vegetarian. I think I want to try that."

"What? She's vegetarian? How do you know that?"

"She told me about some documentaries. I was just watching one. Have you ever seen how they process chicken? Don't even ask me about the cows. It's totally gross. And we're like, eating their terror, you know? Did you know that milk is full of puss and infection?"

"I don't know if that is true."

"It is. You should watch this." He indicates his laptop, and when I glance at the offered screen, I see the image of a cow, its eyes rolling in fear.

"When did you talk about all of this?"

"At dinner."

"Oh. When was that?"

He looks at me like I'm stupid. "I don't know. A couple days ago. You know, at Johnny's."

"Oh, that's right. I forgot." I let out a long breath. "So, vegetarian? I could make pasta, I guess."

"That sounds great."

The garage door begins to ratchet up, and I smile, a quiver on my lips. "Sounds like your dad's home." I stand, and he replaces his earbud, unpausing the documentary that Birdie recommended.

I cannot go downstairs. Not yet. I cannot face him. Instead, I head into the bathroom and turn on the shower, tears running down my face.

Fury returns at my tears. I'm an idiot to be crying because he made love to her. Because he took her to my favorite restaurant. Because my son thinks she is cool and that I am not. I pull off my clothes and step into the stream of water, my hands pressed against my eye sockets to stop the flood of images.

"WHAT WOULD YOU THINK of catering from Pickles for the party?" Chase asks later that night when we are lying in bed. My back is to him. I pretended to be asleep when he came to bed, but now I open my eyes and stare out at the black sky beyond the window.

"Sure. I like Pickles. Their bread is good." I'm relieved that my voice is steady. I flip onto my back. "How many people this year?"

"Twenty, maybe thirty. But you don't have to worry about it. I'll have Birdie arrange for the food."

"Why would you have Birdie arrange for the food?" My voice breaks.

"What difference does it make?"

"It's *my* job. It's the one thing I get to do for the company, Chase." Tears spring into my eyes, and I swipe at them before they can fall.

"Why are you so upset?"

I can feel him turning to look at me, and I hold myself frozen. "I'm not upset. I just don't understand. I have always handled the food for the company party."

"Fine. You can handle the food."

"Fine. Any special diets I need to consider?" I ask, remembering the documentary Birdie encouraged Jackson to watch.

"No. Nothing, really."

"Isn't Birdie vegetarian?" I finally turn to look at him.

His jaw compresses, and he blinks twice. "I don't know. Is she?"

"According to Jackson, she is. Said she gave him a list of food documentaries to watch."

His lips twitch into a quick smile.

"He's decided he's going to try it."

He chuckles. "Why don't you pick up some steaks for the weekend? We'll nip that shit in the bud." He faces me, his eyes soft in the moonlight. He lifts on an elbow and kisses me briefly before settling back, rolling away from me and mumbling, "Good night."

I am wide awake.

# Chapter 24

By the second week in October, Carmen and I still haven't heard anything from the prison. I've incorporated Carmen's cover story into my thoughts, which makes the whole thing more manageable, but I'm still unsettled. The day the maid service is scheduled to deep clean the house before the party, I take the opportunity to drive downtown after work. I hate being in the house when other people are cleaning, feeling lazy while they work. I park in front of Pickles and go inside to get their catering menu. It smells so good that I place an order for tonight to pick up at four, which gives me an hour.

I leave my iPhone in the car then walk down the block to the newspaper office. "Hi. I'd like to look through the archives," I say to the large woman at the front desk.

"Yes, of course. Follow me." She rises and leads me further into the building. She struggles to breathe on the short trek to the computer bay, her legs shifting like tree trunks in a storm, the top half of her body tilting with the effort of motion. She is helpful and smiling, and I feel bad for making her walk.

It takes almost the whole hour to make copies of all the articles relating to the Michael Dietz murder. Two detectives are mentioned multiple times in the articles. One must be the officer who spoke with *Just InJustice*. I make a mental note to look through the Aldrich Police website to see if either Detective Young or Detective Ingram are still on the force. I'll have to wait until I get back to school.

On a whim, I type Chase Reddick into the search bar and wait. The machine churns and finally produces a high school graduation list and his father's obituary. I'm disappointed but not surprised. I was hoping to find something else—a run-in with the law that would explain why he wanted out of town, why else he might've needed an alibi. I want there to be some simple explanation that doesn't include the father of my son being a murderer. Not for Chase's sake but for Jackson's. All week, I've warred against my anger about the video, about the life we share. If I'm lucky, the affair will hold the explosion off a while longer. If he is being satisfied, he is less likely to lose his temper with me.

My mind whirls as I make my way back down the block to pick up my order from Pickles. If I can accept Chase using me as a murder alibi as the reason he crashed back into my life, then maybe I can move on. But if he just needed me to tell the police he had been with me all night, I don't understand our last fifteen years together or why he followed me to New York to begin with. I know he hated working for his dad, but that hardly seemed like enough. Maybe it was all about Dietz. The police couldn't get his DNA as easily if he wasn't in the area.

*Of course. He wanted to be away from the investigation. Then we had Jackson.* Chase loves his son. He felt a responsibility to stay. He's a decent father, even if he isn't a decent husband. Not to me anyway. I see the video again, his hands caressing her hips, his mouth on hers.

He never loved me, not the way a man should love his wife. I know that now, after watching him with Birdie. He was so tender with her. With me, he's always been rough. He never whispered to me the way he purred to her as he thrusted. I am just the ladder he stood on to make himself taller.

To kill time, I drive slowly past the small stucco house where I grew up. A woman and a little girl swing on the front porch. The woman looks up. For a moment, I want to stop, to step onto the familiar porch and tell her that I used to live here when my mother was alive. Longing fills me as I imagine walking through the front door and seeing the dining room where she sat with her morning coffee, the cigarette smoke hanging like a fog above her. I wish I could sit between the mother and daughter on the swing, lay my head on the woman's shoulder, and be comforted. Tears spring to my eyes.

The road curves, and I bide my time, driving through neighborhoods and past strip malls until I think the cleaning people will be gone. By the time I reach our house, our car is enveloped by the scents of bread and meat.

I send a text to Chase. *I brought home Pickles for dinner. I picked up their catering menu. We can look at it tonight.*

*Cool.*

I breathe. I've covered myself in case he questions my traitorous phone's report of my whereabouts.

# Chapter 25

It looks like rain the evening of the company party, but despite thick clouds and the wind whipping through the trees, it holds off. We've hosted the party for years, and many of the men and their wives are familiar to me. Costumes are optional—it's not quite Halloween—but a few, like me and Chase, go all out. My hair is hidden under a frizzed-out wig, and the lame golden disco getup is flared at the wrists and legs, a complement to Chase's white leisure suit with golden trim. We greet our guests together.

Birdie is one of the last to arrive. I have stepped away from Chase to run another pitcher of margaritas, and when I come back, she is standing in the foyer beside him. I keep them in sight, waiting for them to touch, but she breezes past him after the barest of greetings and joins one of the wives on the sofa.

*What a smooth operator.* I fill two more glasses before I reach her.

"Margarita?" I offer with my best smile.

"Yes, please." She stands and accepts a glass.

"What are you tonight?" I gesture to her spiked hair and studded leather mini dress.

"Punk rocker." She throws one arm up and sticks out her tongue, emulating youth and disrespect.

"Nice." I nod, my wig bouncing. "I don't think we've met."

"I'm Birdie." She extends her hand, but I shrug, my hands full with the cups and pitcher.

I knew she would be here, but I had not been prepared for her to be so relaxed. She doesn't even have the decency to look guilty.

"It's good to meet you finally," I continue. "I feel like I should know you, as much as Chase talks about you." He doesn't talk about her any more than he talks about any of the rest of the crew, but I am gratified to see the blush rising to her cheeks.

*Caught ya.* I smile, then I turn to my other guests, giving niceties like "How are you?" and "I'm so glad you were able to get a sitter" and "How old are the twins now?" and "Isn't that nice" and all the other bullshit conversation that comes with being the boss's wife. I steer our guests to the dining room, where the Pickles buffet is laid out. Jackson comes down and takes a sandwich on his way out the door to spend the night with Dalton. I remind him to keep his phone on and to let me know if he needs anything.

Chase and I intersect from time to time, but mostly, we move through the crowd independently. I smile, laugh, and refill drinks, watching for any points of connection between Chase and Birdie, but they are discreet.

When the party begins to break apart, I start clearing away the debris as Chase sees our guests out. He is gone for a long time, and when I look out onto the street, I see one car left with no sign of Chase. I move through the house and step onto the back deck, collecting stray cups and plates.

"Shh."

The sound comes from below the deck, in the sheltered area outside of the basement door.

Muffled giggles. "Shhh."

I turn back into the house and close the door as if I didn't hear. I finish in the kitchen, and when I come through the living room, I see Chase out front, holding Birdie's car door for her. I yank off the ridiculous wig and leave it with the rest of the mess before going upstairs to shower.

*Bold little bitch.*

# Chapter 26

A couple of days after the party, I hide out in my bathroom, my burner phone in my hand, waiting on Carmen's reply. Something inside of me has changed. It's not that I want away from Chase so much now as I want to see him suffer. To go to prison and feel powerless. That damn video just runs through my head. *Why couldn't he ever once treat me like that?*

When he came to bed after the party, I rolled over to look at him. "You might want to check the lock on the basement door."

"Why's that?"

"I thought I heard somebody down there tonight while you were walking everybody out."

"Okay. I'll check that." But he didn't get out of bed and go down the stairs. Of course he didn't. He knew who was down there, and so do I.

I hate him so much.

"Delilah!"

I jump and drop the secret phone onto the floor.

"Where are you?"

*How did I not hear the garage door? Shit. Shit.* I try to remember if I locked the bathroom door at least.

After stashing the phone back into its hiding spot, I pull down my pants and sit on the toilet. Folding forward, I call out, "I'm in the bathroom!"

I wipe, flush, and drop the lid on the toilet, hoping it's loud enough for him to hear. Running water, I scrub my hands, my heart jackhammering in my chest. When I open the door, he is lounging at the entrance to the bedroom.

"You all right?" he asks, pushing off the door frame with his shoulder before coming into the room and walking toward me. "You look pale. You sick?"

"No. I'm fine." I turn off the light. "You're home early."

"Yeah. We finished that house on Broad Street. Thought I'd take you out for dinner. That Mediterranean place you like."

"Oh. That would be great." I cross my arms over my chest and move away from the bathroom door. "How'd the house turn out?"

"It's good. I think we'll clear a good profit from it."

I nod and angle past him through the bedroom door, into the hall.

He follows me. "Where's Jack?"

"He's at Dalton's. They're playing basketball. I can call him. Have him come home."

I've reached the top of the stairs, but before I can take that first step, he catches my wrist and turns me toward him. "We'll pick him up on the way." He leans into me, trying to catch my eyes. "You seem strange. You okay?"

"I'm fine." I offer a small smile but cannot make eye contact.

"So we have the house to ourselves?" He pulls me close, and I force myself not to push away. "Come back to the bedroom."

THE RESTAURANT IS LOUD. The exposed ductwork in the ceiling is cool and trendy but does not improve the acoustics. I smile at Chase when he speaks to me, trying to figure out his change in demeanor. It's almost the way it was when I first came home, the way it always is after a beatdown. *What is he making up for?* Maybe he thinks I saw Birdie's email.

I don't know what he knows, so I let him lead. I play along, filling in the picture of our happy little family.

"Oh, hey!" Jackson's exuberance draws my eyes from the menu to discover the source of his outburst. My heart stalls in my chest. Birdie's hand is on Jackson's shoulder, but her eyes are on Chase. She turns her attention from Chase to me, and in the shifting, I see her arm flung over her face, telling him "no" in the moment before he walked, bare-assed, across the room.

"Oh, hey, Birdie. What are you doing here?" Her name sounds like a song on Chase's tongue, familiar.

"Just came by to pick up dinner." She looks toward Jackson then to me, a smile lifting the corners of her pretty mouth. "Good to see you again, Delilah."

Leaning back in my chair, I raise my eyebrows like this is a true coincidence. "What a nice surprise."

"Yeah. I love this place." She and Jackson share an intricate handshake with snaps and slaps. "How are you, Jack?"

"Great."

"Oh, yeah. I forgot how you know Jackson. You're that badass Krav Maga chick." For a moment, I think my words are lost as Chase stands and grabs a chair from a neighboring table and invites her to join us.

"Yeah. I started Krav Maga when I was twelve, I guess. Self-defense is important." She casually accepts the offered seat as she answers.

I am floored as she joins us at the table like an old friend of the family. Chase has placed her between himself and Jackson, across from me. *What does this whore think she's doing?*

"Yes, it is." I have no other option than to continue playing along.

Chase finally glances toward me. Apparently satisfied by my act, he smiles, takes his seat, then motions for the waitress. I clench my jaw as Birdie says that he doesn't need to add her to our ticket.

She pulls out her wallet, extracts a card, and lays it on the table. "I'll buy my own."

"Nonsense." Chase picks up the Mastercard and holds it like a flag. She acquiesces and takes the card from Chase, but not before I glimpse the name on it. *Bridget Dietz.*

My lips move incoherently as my mind races. *Dietz? Like Michael Dietz? Are they family?* I force myself to close my mouth.

Birdie offers a nervous laugh at Chase's grand gesture and glances again at me, a flush rising on her cheeks. "No, really, I can't. You're having dinner with your family. I don't want to intrude."

Maybe she *does* have a soul. I lock eyes with her. "No, please. Join us."

"Are you sure?" She settles into her chair.

"Of course." I look up at Chase, and he winks at me. "How are you feeling about payroll?" I ask, trying for a conversational tone.

She nods, smiles, then glances at Chase. "Good. It's good."

"I was really surprised when he told me you were going to be taking that on. He must really trust you."

It feels dangerous to speak to her. I can't be certain if they're onto me. I doubt this meeting was an accident. I try to stay in the conversation, to hold my own against this usurper, but soon, they are talking about Krav Maga and the house on Broad Street that Birdie "just loves."

After the initial shock of seeing her has worn off, I let my mind embrace her presence. Maybe their dinner plan was what inspired his attentions to me earlier. It could be some kind of sick turn-on for Chase to think about dining with his wife and his lover. My appetite disappears as I watch him with her, speaking with his mouth full. He glances at me, midsentence, as his hand slips beneath the table to touch her.

*Fucking animal.* He must think I am a fool. I participate in their conversation when I must and pretend to be oblivious. My skin becomes less opaque as the meal goes on. My mind spins. *I could just let him go.*

My skin is so thin by the time we leave the restaurant that I am surprised when the hostess smiles at me.

"Well, I'll see you at the office," Chase says to Birdie, and she peels away from our group before turning, smiling, with eyes that are only for him.

"Thanks for dinner. It was great to see you, Delilah. You should join us at Krav Maga."

I wish I was looking at Chase when she said that. I imagine his eyes growing round at the thought. I imagine him trying to send her the message that he does not want me there.

"Maybe I'll do that. Self-defense is important, right?"

"You said it, sister." She winks.

Had I known the life in store for me, I would have learned self-defense and how to handle a gun. I would have walked away from him at the Warehouse and lived an entirely different life. Maybe I can pass him over to her and wish her the best. After all, Chase called her a badass. She might be able to hold her own against him.

I replay the evening, from the moment she walked in to the wink as she left. "What's her last name?" I ask, trying to sound normal. I know what I saw, but it was so quick I doubt myself.

"Dietz," he says, pulling out onto the street, looking satisfied and proud.

"Didn't we go to school with a kid named Dietz?"

"Yeah. Mike."

"That's right. Any relation?" I feel my skin thickening to its normal density.

"Yeah, brother. She doesn't talk about him."

"Why not?"

He glances at me then looks back at the road. "He's dead. Pissed off the wrong guy and got beaten to death with his own bat."

None of the articles or websites specified he was killed with his own bat. They all said the murder weapon, a blunt object, was unrecovered. The night Michael Dietz died, Chase collected a bat from the bushes as we walked to his apartment. In a flash, I see the bat in our basement, rolling in an arc on the concrete floor. The initials O.W. were carved into the knob. It rotates, and the block letters flip. *M.O.?* Not *O* but *D*. I gasp, understanding.

"You okay?"

"Yeah. Just a stitch. I think I ate too much." I press my hand against my ribs and breathe. *We have the murder weapon in the basement.* But I don't understand why he would get close to the sister of the boy he killed.

"She's nice." I lean back in my seat and let him think that I'm too stupid to know what he has done. Any of what he has done.

## Chapter 27

Mike Dietz isn't the only person involved in that night who has a little sister. Dabney Holt has one as well. If I can't meet Holt himself, I can at least meet with his sister.

It's not detective work to find her name on the website Justice for Dabney Holt and Michael Dietz. There have been no changes to the site since I first found it. I'm afraid the point of contact will be a dead end, unmonitored after nearly fifteen years, but I send an email from my secret phone and hope.

I pick up Jackson from basketball practice, and we drive home. Chase is working late, so I have an hour before I'll have to take Jackson to the Krav Maga studio. While I fold the clothes from the dryer then transfer the wet ones to tumble, I wait for the burner phone to vibrate. Emboldened, I go downstairs, sitting at the kitchen table while Jackson is upstairs.

Finally, it buzzes with the email from Desirey Harrison. *I'm in Drake now. We could meet at the McDonald's.*

I used the cover story about Cheryl Buxton considering Holt's story for a future project. Drake is just a few miles down the road from Aldrich. I send her a time, and we are set. I slide the phone into my purse, hiding it under all my crap.

Using my iPhone, I text Chase, *Do you want me to feed Jackson before class? I'm going to have dinner with Carmen.*

He doesn't respond. I don't even get dots. It makes me anxious, like he knows I am sneaking around. Jackson solves the dilemma of whether I should feed him by coming down and fixing a turkey sandwich for himself. I offer sides, but he isn't interested, and he finishes his sandwich as we drive toward the studio.

Chase texts while we are in the car. *We'll grab something on the way home if he's hungry. Are you on the way?*

I don't respond because we are already pulling into the lot. Jackson is out of the car before I can tell him to have fun. I watch him make his way into the studio. Chase's truck roars beside mine, and he points his finger at me like a gun. I pull into a nearby empty spot, but before I can get out, another car parks beside Chase. I watch as the pretty little bird flaps out of her car and skips toward his truck.

Chase tilts his head in warning. Her eyes cut to me, then she smiles, shifting her trajectory in such a seamless fashion that it almost doesn't seem like he was the original destination. My feet touch the asphalt, and she stops in front of me.

"You gonna join us?"

"Oh, God, no." I am impressed by her ability to change gears, by her brazenness. They both must think I'm totally clueless, as if I can't see it written all over his face that he is screwing her.

"Where are you going to dinner with Carmen?" Chase asks as he joins us.

"I don't know. We're just catching up."

"Like you don't see enough of each other while you're playing library." He puckers his lips, the way he does when he is mocking me.

"We don't get to talk at school."

Not that he actually cares about me or my plans. They are standing so near one another that no light passes between them.

"Whatever." He shrugs. "Jack inside?" I nod, and he turns to Birdie. "Shall we?"

"Sure. It was good to see you," she says to me.

"Yeah, you too..." *You sly little thing.* "Kick his ass," I say just to her, barely a whisper.

"You know I will." She winks as if we are on a team.

I slide into my car and watch them all the way across the parking lot, expecting to see the moment they touch, but his hand does not float to her back, her shoulder does not bump against him. He merely opens the door for her, and she gives him the prettiest smile as she ducks under his arm. My stomach pitches.

DESIREY HARRISON IS tall with long brown hair piled into a messy bun at the top of her head. I know she is Holt's sister as soon as she walks through the door. The family resemblance is strong, not just in her height but also in the angle of her eyes. I rise from my plastic seat to catch her attention.

"Are you Sue?" she asks as I cross the dining area. I told her my name was Sue Stone—Suzanne is my middle name. Delilah stands out too much, and I had to be careful in case she mentioned to someone else that she was meeting with me.

"I am. Thank you for meeting me." We shake hands. "Want coffee?" I ask, offering to step to the counter on her behalf.

"No. I'm good."

"Great. Shall we sit?"

We make our way to the table, where my coffee is still steaming.

"We came across your brother's story on *Just InJustice*." I jump in with both feet, using the storyline Carmen fabricated. "You know, they put out a pretty strong case that he's not the guy."

"He's not. Anybody who knows Dabs knows he couldn't have done this." Her lips fold down.

"Why not? What about him says that?"

"Dabs couldn't have hurt anybody. He just wasn't that kind of kid." She meets my eyes with a cold expression that feels like a challenge.

It's like pulling teeth. "What kind of kid was he?"

"Why are you interested in this?" She leans back in her chair and folds her arms across her chest.

"I told you, I'm part of Cheryl Buxton's advance team. She wants to write a book about him. I've made a request to visit him, but I'm still waiting for authorization. Ms. Buxton is impatient to get started. So we'd like to understand who he was before that night." I made as much clear in my email.

"What's her angle? Does she think he did it?" The closed look in her eyes begins to make sense. She needs to know if I already have my mind made up.

"No." I stop short of telling her the truth of why I don't think he did it. "She thinks he was railroaded in a snap judgement. The police were pressured to produce a suspect, and the DA was pushed to rush to trial because the university, and the town, really, had a lot to lose if the case went unsolved."

"So she wants to write about corruption? Make my brother to be a stooge?"

I hadn't expected her to be uncooperative. If Dabney were my brother, I would want his name cleared. "No. We want to find out the truth, and if he didn't do it, we want to tell his story."

She nods but does not speak. I'm not sure if I set her off somehow, but I sense she's about to get up and walk away. I have to dangle another carrot.

"I have kind of a personal interest in this case."

"How's that?"

"I went to high school over in Drake. I graduated with Mike. We didn't really know each other. I was only there for my senior year. I don't remember much about the investigation, you know, and you'd think I would, it happening so close to home and all. But it was over so quickly. They had an arrest before the investigation even started, really. Arrested, convicted, and sentenced before the next semester. When I ran across the *InJustice* story, I thought they made a strong case for his innocence."

"It *was* all over really quick."

"How thorough could they have been? How long was it before he was convicted?" I try to build some sort of comradery with her.

"Not quite three months."

"That's what I mean. Did they even talk to anybody else?"

"I have the witness list. They talked to a hundred people. But there were no other suspects." The expression in her eyes shifts, and I think I've passed a test.

"Well, there should have been. Other suspects, I mean. How many people were at that house party? What about the people across the street at the bar? Any one of them could have done it."

"They talked to everybody that night. Nobody seemed to know anything."

"They didn't talk to me that night. I had to go down to the station the next day to give my statement."

She looks at me like she isn't sure how to process my words.

"I was at the bar. When I left, I saw the police cars and an ambulance, but the police didn't stop me. Who else could have come through the bar and walked away?"

"I don't know. I thought they locked it down." She leans forward, suddenly more interested.

"Not until after they loaded him into the ambulance. At least an hour after he was found, as far as I can tell. Why didn't they close it down immediately? Why didn't they come over and at least get a list of everybody? If they didn't talk to me, who else did they miss?" It may have been a mistake to mention being on the witness list. Delilah Stone is on the list, but not Sue Stone.

"Did you see anything?"

"My friends and I walked to the bar, so we could have seen the killer going into the house."

"Did you?"

"I don't know. But they didn't ask me. They asked if I knew the victim or your brother and if I had ever bought illegal drugs. They didn't ask if I saw anything."

"That night? They asked if you knew my brother that night?" Her voice rises with incredulity, walking a ridge toward irritation.

"Not that night. The next day, though. They already had Dabney pegged as their guy."

"Who else could've walked away while they were focused on my brother?" Anger flares in her eyes and stalls, simmering.

"Who knows? Surely, we weren't the only ones."

"We?"

I am so proud of her for catching it that I could cheer. I said it so it would sound like a slip. "What?"

"We. You just said 'we.' Was there more than just you?"

"I was with my boyfriend. I dragged him to the police station the next day. He said they asked him the same questions," I say, letting it hang, hoping she will ask about Chase.

She doesn't disappoint. "What did he say?"

"He told them that he didn't know either of them and denied ever buying illegal drugs. None of which was true. I found out later that he did know your brother and Dietz, and I'd be really surprised if he hadn't bought illegal drugs." I sigh.

"You think your boyfriend had something to do with it?" she whispers across the table, leaning toward me.

"I don't know about that, but it just seems like such shoddy police work. If they did any kind of investigation at all, it seems that they would have discovered that he lied about knowing the suspect and victim. If they were seriously looking for somebody else, my boyfriend would have been a person of interest at least." I shouldn't have said that last part and cover it quickly. "They missed us leaving the bar and never would have talked to us at all if we hadn't gone down there. Who else did they miss and not bother looking for?"

"I don't know." She shakes her head, but the excitement in her eyes is just what I hoped for. I've given her enough to think I am a lifeline.

"I think they made him a scapegoat, and that's what Cheryl wants to write. His exoneration."

The tension in her face lessens, and she exhales a long breath.

"What was your brother like before that night?" I ask as if that is really what I am interested in, not like I just came to make her talk her brother into letting us visit.

"He was the kind of kid who rescued rabbits from our dog. Everybody called him to get cats down from trees. He has a kind heart." Her eyes soften with memories of the boy her brother used to be.

"What about the drugs? Was he different when he was on drugs?"

"It wasn't like he was a druggie. He experimented, but it wasn't a regular thing. I don't really know what he was like when he was on drugs, but nobody at that party said he seemed aggressive."

"What do you know about that night?"

"He got some LSD. He was hallucinating. It was a bad trip. He said that it was raining but not on him. Said there were snakes everywhere."

"He got the LSD from Dietz?"

"Yep. He was messed up."

I don't know much about LSD, but this is the story *Just InJustice* had told, so I'm not surprised. "What happened then?"

"He went back to Dietz to ask for help. He wanted something to counteract the effects of the LSD. That's when he found him. He said he thought it was all part of the hallucination. He didn't think it was real."

"And then?"

"According to him, he went back to the party and started telling everybody to check on Dietz."

"Why 'according to him'?" I'm puzzled.

"Everybody said he was crying, talking gibberish. Nobody could really understand what he was saying."

Just as we are making headway, my skin prickles, and I straighten. I am being watched. Chills erupt on my spine, and I look through the windows and see a man I don't know standing on the other side of the glass. He is looking in, not at me, past me, around me. Searching for someone. His eyes stop at us. He lifts his phone to the window. Desirey follows my gaze.

"You know him?" I ask.

She waves at the window. "That's my husband. Just making sure you are legit."

"Did he take my picture?" I can't keep the edge out of my voice.

"Yeah. But he won't show anybody, and he'll delete it when I come home."

"Seriously?" It seems insane. What does he think I might do to her?

"You'd be surprised at the crazies we've been approached by."

"I guess so." I wouldn't have thought anybody would approach them about a fifteen-year-old murder. "Why did you agree to meet me? If you thought I might be a crazy."

"I meet with a lot of people who might be crazy. I love my brother. I want him to get his life back. He didn't kill that guy, but he's wasting away in prison anyway." She gives the man a thumbs-up, and he turns, walking swiftly into the parking lot.

I cannot pull my eyes from the window, trying to place whether her husband looked familiar. If he knows Chase, he might tell him that I was here, meeting with his wife about the Dietz murder. "Nobody can know I am here. This has to be quiet until Cheryl is ready to launch." My voice cracks in the uptick, and I hear my hysteria. I rein myself in.

"We won't tell anybody." Her hand touches mine on the table, as if she thinks I am about to bolt. "We've just been really vocal about thinking there's a murderer out there. We have to be prepared for that person to make contact to shut us up." She leans forward, letting her voice barely whisper across the table. "We have to be careful."

A shiver rolls through my body, and I tug my hand free, lifting it to touch my scar. *Me too.* I do not dare to say the words aloud.

I look down at my notes to try and remember where we were. "So, nobody went and checked on Dietz?"

"Well, yeah. Finally, somebody did. That's when they called the police."

"What was your brother doing then?"

"I don't know. Crying. Seeing snakes. He was still high. He doesn't really remember what he did."

"When did the police first talk to him?"

She drops her voice, as if this is a truth better left unspoken. "That night."

"But he was high." My jaw drops. Surely, they wouldn't question him about something like that when he was impaired.

"Pfft. They didn't care."

"He was a good target." I agree.

"Yeah, he couldn't say for sure what he had done, and he had blood on his hands."

"He did? I hadn't heard that."

"Well, not his hands, really, just a spot on the end of his pointer finger. He must have touched Dietz trying to wake him."

"Why didn't that information make it into the trial?"

"Did you see what Dietz looked like? Whoever did it would have had more than that. The spot supported Dabs's story, but his attorney didn't want to introduce it."

"Why not?"

"He thought putting the idea that he had blood on his hands would seal the case, that that's all they would hear." As she talks, I become more convinced that her brother was a scapegoat, even without my vested interest.

We sit for a long minute while I process the information, reframing my understanding of the case. My mind is spinning. Maybe somebody from the party will remember seeing Chase in the house. Then it wouldn't just be me going to the police. Maybe, if I can stir the pot enough, somebody else will make that call, and I won't even have to talk to Dabney Holt. "I'd love to see your witness list."

"I'll send it to you."

"That would be great." After a beat, I add, "Maybe you could put a word in for us with your brother—so he knows we're legit." I intentionally use her word.

"Sure, I'll do that."

I wonder if I've convinced her that I'm not a crackpot. We talk a little longer, but I am excited to get the list and start the work of cross-referencing with my yearbook.

On my way back to Aldrich, the list pings into my alter ego's inbox. I drive a little faster than I should, needing to see it but unwilling to take my eyes off the road.

When I pull into my spot in the driveway, I'm relieved that Chase isn't home. I will have a few minutes alone.

I pull my iPhone from my purse and check it. I've missed a text from him, and my chest heaves.

*McDonald's?* He sent it twenty minutes ago.

I sit in the car and text back.

*We just had coffee. You out for dinner? Maybe I'll join you.*

*We're done. Almost home.*

I can't tell if he sounds angry. I walk toward the house, catching sight of Bruce in his window. I smile and wave, putting on a show.

I rush through the house and return my secret phone to its hiding place just in time to hear the garage door going up.

# Chapter 28

After the kids file into to their classrooms for the morning, Carmen and I investigate in the library. We compare Desirey's list to my high school yearbook and put a small red *x* beside the names we find in both. We also mark who we remember seeing at the Warehouse with a circle, all kids we knew from college, not high school. The party seemed to be a townie gathering. I draw a line through the names of people we were with—me and Chase, Carmen, Chloe, and Sharla. That's five people from the mile-long list we will not need to look up.

We make quick work of it, then Carmen takes the yearbook and the list back to her office, where nobody is tracking keystrokes. I churn through the day, shelving books, helping students.

THE NEXT DAY, CHASE works late, and Jackson asks to study at Dalton's house. I let Chase know I'll be dropping Jackson off and ask if he needs anything from the store. He doesn't. I hope my excuse buys me enough time.

I tuck my iPhone snugly between the sofa cushions before leaving. Only the secret phone is in my purse. Chase will be angry if he texts and I don't respond, but I take the risk. He's checking in less these days because of Birdie.

Carmen and I have split our new list to cover more ground—she is starting with the police, and I'm starting with the townies. With Chase's friendships on the force, she agreed it would be best if I steer clear. It's still a risk, talking to townies, but Chase is preoccupied, and my anger gives me strength.

After dropping off Jackson, I park on the square and walk the block to Haynes Body Shop. Don Haynes was one of the witnesses the night of the murder. I remember him from high school, and I'm almost certain he wasn't at the Warehouse. As a townie, he wouldn't have missed that party.

"I'm Sue Stone. I called earlier."

"Yeah. I got your message."

"Thank you for meeting with me. I'm gathering information for Cheryl Buxton, the author. She's considering writing about the Michael Dietz murder."

Don is wiry and swipes a lock of black hair off his forehead before offering a me a calloused hand. "I don't really know anything about it."

"You were on the witness list."

"Ah. Well, yeah, but that doesn't mean nothing."

"Can I ask you a few questions?" I feel like I should take off the ball cap, but I don't. I don't want him to have a clear idea of what I look like. I learned my lesson with Desirey and her photographing husband.

He shrugs then ushers me into his office.

After I take a seat, I look down at my notebook, eyeing my first question. "Where were you that night?"

"I was at the house where it happened."

"Were you familiar with Michael Dietz?"

"Sure. He was a good kid. A little wild, but we all were. He didn't deserve what he got."

"Did you know Dabney Holt?"

He nods, puckering his lips.

"Do you think he did this?" I hadn't planned to open like that, but now that the question is out, I'm relieved.

"The police thought so. Dabs was a big guy—kinda soft, though. I wouldn't have thought he'd do something like that, but Dietz was good at pushing buttons."

"What kind of buttons could he push?"

"Everybody has a trigger. Holt wasn't very smart, and if I remember right, he was a little sensitive about it."

"You think Dietz picked on him?"

"Yeah. Everybody picked on Holt. He didn't really mind so much."

"He didn't mind being bullied?" I remember Jackson shrugging when he talked about Heather, saying it was "just her way." But then he exploded on her.

"It wasn't like that. We all liked him. He was just different. Kinda slow, you know?"

I look back at my list and pick up where we left off. "Did you feel like Dietz and Holt were friends?"

"I don't know. I guess so."

I pull out the yearbook. "If I point out a couple of people, would you mind telling me if you remember seeing them there that night?"

"Oh, hell. That was a hundred years ago." He blows out a long breath, and I catch the hint of his last cigarette.

"Will you try?"

He agrees, and I point to several of the headshots I've marked with an *x*. He narrows the five down to three. I ask if the three he remembers from the house are still in the area, and he tells me two are, but one is dead. After I make a note of their names, I point to one last face, Chase's.

"I don't know. He was usually there, but I don't remember seeing him that night. It was Friday—he didn't usually show at Friday parties."

"Do you know if he's still in town?" I can't let him see that Chase Reddick is the only card I am interested in.

"Yeah. Works construction. But you know he wouldn'a had anything to do with it."

"Why not?"

"Well, just doesn't seem likely." He drops his voice. "Dietz got all his stuff from Reddick. Reddick worked Drake, and Dietz worked Aldrich. That's how it was."

"What does that mean?" I'm not following.

"They were partners, man."

"Oh." *They were partners?* "Are you suggesting that Reddick was dealing drugs?"

"Yeah. That was kinda common knowledge. I think the police were getting ready to bust them—that's why Reddick skipped town."

*Oh my God! How did I get caught up with him?* I didn't know anything about drugs except that he occasionally smoked some weed.

I fight to process this new information while keeping the momentum going. "You're saying he left town because he was going to get caught dealing drugs?" Or because he killed Dietz.

"Well, I don't know that for a fact. That's just how we all figured it after Dietz died, and they were looking around at his connections. Them two were tight as ticks."

"Interesting." I hadn't gotten the impression from Chase. Of course, I hadn't seen much of him between my freshman and senior year.

Don shrugs. "You could ask him. He took over his dad's construction company. He's still in town."

Finally certain he doesn't recognize me, the tension in my shoulders drops. "Seems to have straightened himself out, then. We all grow up," I add as if I know about living a wild youth.

"I reckon we do." He nods.

"I'll see if he'll meet with me. Thanks for your help." We shake hands.

After reminding Don to keep the details of our meeting confidential—I use some bogus legalese about protecting Cheryl's copyright—I check my secret phone. I missed a call from a woman named Renae, who was returning my message. I call her back while I am still in the parking lot.

"Could we meet somewhere?" I ask.

"I can't get away today. I'm watching my sister's kids."

"I'll come to you if that would work."

She agrees, and I type the address into the GPS. It's close. I should have plenty of time before Chase gets home.

REYNOLD'S DRIVE WAS the nice part of town when we were growing up. It still is, but the homes are old now, dated.

Renae leads me past three children glued to the television and into the kitchen, where she offers coffee. Cup in hand, I sit at the table then slip the list of witnesses from my envelope.

"You're writing a book?"

"No, not me. I work for Cheryl Buxton—you know, the author of *The Raven's Song*."

She pushes her lips out and shrugs. "Not much of a reader."

"Well, I'm not a writer for sure." I laugh, trying to find a connecting point. "I'm just part of her advance team. She's trying to decide if there is anything about Dietz's case to write about."

She takes the list and looks down it. Finding her name, she shakes her head as if remembering why she was questioned. "That was a terrible night."

"What can you tell me?"

"I went to the party with Tom Lassiter and Mindy McCall." She points out their names on my list.

The name Tom Lassiter jars me. I remember him from high school. He and Chase were tight. I hadn't even recognized his name on the list and feel the near escape in that I hadn't tried to call him yet. *That would have been bad.*

Smiling, I take a moment to mark all three of their names with an *h* for house party.

"We were in the living room," she continues. "Well, Mindy and I were. I don't know where Tom had got himself off to." She shrugs, and I encourage her to continue. "The music was really loud, just thumping. We'd all been laughing at Dabs—he was tripping, walking on his tiptoes so he wouldn't step on snakes. He was a funny guy."

"He was funny?" Nobody else had mentioned that.

"Not always, but that night, he was. Maybe we just thought he was funny cause we were high."

"What were you on?"

"Oh, just pot. Nothing major. But, you know, sometimes it makes things look funny that aren't."

"Yeah." That hadn't been my experience. The few times I smoked with Chase, it made me anxious and worried.

"I'm trying to figure out who was at the house and who was at the bar." I hand over the list again.

She scans it, frowning. "I don't even know most of these people."

"I brought the Drake yearbook. Thought it might be helpful." I slide it from my bag and let her take her time flipping through the pages, pointing out people she remembered being there. I hold my breath while she is on Chase's page.

She flips to the next page, and I exhale, disappointed.

Then she flips back. "I think this guy was at the party. He usually was, but I don't remember seeing him that night." Her finger lands on Chase's face. "He never really stuck around."

As if I don't know him, I crane my neck to see the name beneath the picture she is touching. "Chase Reddick?" Finding his name on the list of witnesses, I write an *h* beside it too. Renae points to several other photos, and I make the same mark. When I see Carmen tomorrow, we'll cross-reference our materials and see what the shape of the picture is then.

"You're not sure if this Chase Reddick was there?"

"Like I said, I don't remember for sure, but Mindy would. She had a thing for him. He was a townie." Her eyes widen as she whispers, "Had a big dick."

My face blazes. "Excuse me?"

"They were a thing for a while. I wonder whatever happened to him."

*I don't care,* I tell myself, but I know I'm lying. I ask if she happens to know how I could get in touch with Mindy, and she gives me her number. I write it down in my notebook.

I turn back to the paper, refocusing her attention. "Hmm." I add a question mark beside the *h* I've just written. "I wonder if he's still in town. Were he and Mike friends? Is that why he would have been there? Would he know if Mike was having problems with somebody?"

Chase must stand out in her memory but not because I bungled keeping my poker face over him. She doesn't know, so I go back through the list and ask the same basic questions of the other people she pointed out. I leave the yearbook open to Chase's page and end my questions with him. I want her to continue thinking about Chase—maybe she will call the police and put his name forward so I don't have to.

IN MY CAR, I DIAL THE number Renae gave me for Mindy and leave a message. As I start my car, I glance in the rearview mirror. Someone is parked behind me, smoking a cigarette in the driver's seat. I squint, trying to figure out if the guy looks familiar. Dark hair puffs out over his ears as if he's used to wearing a ball cap. High, sharp cheekbones protrude from beneath deep-set eyes. With the style of his rumpled clothes, I can see that he's younger than I first thought, probably a late teen.

*This is ridiculous.* I'm getting jumpy with my clandestine search. I've been out of reach for too long. I call Carmen and tell her about Mindy.

"That's good. I've got good news too. I have a meeting with Scott Young this Friday—the detective who worked the investigation. He's retired now but said he remembers the case."

"That sounds promising. Can I drop the yearbook off?" I don't really want to drive to her apartment, but I don't want the yearbook and my notes anywhere Chase might see them. She agrees, and twenty minutes later, I finally make it home. Chase and Jackson are not here, and when I get inside and dig through the sofa for my regular phone, I see a text from Chase. *Going out.*

The text came in fifteen minutes ago, and I reply, *Was in the shower. Really tired. Heading to bed.*

# Chapter 29

Mindy Johnson calls me on Wednesday afternoon. I am sitting in the line at Jackson's school, the one time this week that he doesn't have after-school activities or Krav Maga.

I get right to the point, worried that the school will let out before I can finish speaking with her. I've been very bold, carrying my secret phone in my purse.

After my brief introduction about writing a book and following up on leads that the police may have overlooked, I say, "I'm trying to clarify who was at the house and who was at the Warehouse that night. We had a question about somebody that your friend thought you'd remember being at the party."

"She told me. You're talking about Chase Reddick?"

"Yes." This is it. The answer that will make or break my theory. "Was he at the party that night?"

"He was."

"You are sure it was him?"

"Yeah, I wouldn't forget Chase Reddick." There is a bitter tone in her voice—frustration, a wound.

"Why is that?"

"We were dating. Then he just fell off the radar, and two weeks later, he moved to New York with some bitch."

I pause. "You were dating?"

"Yeah. For, like, six months, and then he just dropped me like a bad habit."

"Oh." The understanding is like a clap of thunder, and my ears ring. It wasn't just a fling.

"Yeah." She lets out a sigh. "So, yes, I saw him at the party. We had plans to hook up after."

"Okay. So you spoke?"

"Yes. Well, not in so many words. He was really off—like, cold—so I left him alone." Her voice is so wistful, so full of loss that I wonder if she was in love with him. Chase could be her one that got away. "He was kinda moody, you know?"

"Kinda" doesn't begin to cover it. I shake my head. "Did anybody else see him that night?"

"I don't know." I can almost hear the shrugging. "He was coming down the hall, and I was coming out of the bathroom. I said, 'Hey,' and he just kinda nodded and walked past. Like he didn't even know me. That's the last time I ever spoke to him."

"But you were dating?"

"Yeah. That's what I thought. I don't know what I did to piss him off, but he was done with me." Anger leaches from her words again.

"Did he ever hit you?" I ask, trying to sound offhand.

"What?"

"Did he ever seem violent to you?"

"He never hit me or anything, but he was a little scary. He was an intense dude, could be so sweet, and then bam! Different guy. He was good in bed, though." She gives a small chuckle. "I just never knew what I did wrong. It's always bothered me."

"I'm sure it wasn't you." I don't want to think about Chase and this woman together, but I can't help but wonder if he was tender with her the way he was in the video with Birdie. Before I can spiral further, I ask, "Where did the hall lead?"

"Back door."

"Could he have been going to the room where Dietz was?"

"Well, I guess, but I doubt it."

"Why is that?"

"Mike got all his supply from Chase. They didn't generally like to be seen together. They never held court in the same place."

This corroborates what Don Haynes had said about Chase and Dietz being dealer partners. *Why the hell wasn't Chase the prime suspect?*

"Did you tell the police that?"

"Did I want to die? Oh my God. Chase would have blown me up if I'd told the police he was a drug dealer. Seriously." She inhales deeply, and I imagine her sucking on a cigarette.

"And you thought you were still together at that point, right?"

"Yeah. Right."

"Did you ever know the two of them to have problems?" Just as I get the question out, the afternoon announcements echo from the school, muffled by the brick walls. Jackson will be out any second.

"Chase and Mike?"

"Yeah."

"No. Never really saw them together. Chase liked to keep all the parts of his life separate."

One of the kids near the pickup line screams.

"Chase is still around here, you know," she continues. "You should go ask him, but don't tell him I said he was a drug dealer."

"Oh, no. Your identity will be kept completely confidential, and of course, you can't tell anybody about this conversation. It has to be quiet until Cheryl launches."

"Yeah, what's to tell? I don't know anything."

"All right. Thanks again for your time."

I disconnect and fold my face into my hands, pressing hard against my eye sockets. When I look up again, my hands drag down to cover my mouth. I'll have to compose myself before my son gets in. In a minute, I spot him, coming out of the school in the middle of a pack. *How did I not know who Chase was?*

Jackson fist-bumps a friend and comes to climb into the car.

I can't do this.

# Chapter 30

My nails are bitten to the quick, and the meat around the edges is shredded. *I have to drop it. It's too dangerous.* The thoughts eat me alive as I drop Jackson off on Thursday morning then head to Eastside.

After talking with Mindy, I couldn't sleep over how close I had come to calling Chase's former best friend and how that would have ended. I wasn't far down the list, but I hadn't even thought about who these people were and if any of them were still connected to Chase. Jackson is fourteen. Four more years, and he'll be grown. *I* could survive anything for four years, but I wouldn't put my son through the fallout of this careless investigation.

Last night, I texted Carmen from my secret phone, telling her it was over. It was too dangerous. I haven't checked the phone since, so I do not know if she's responded. I try to catch her in her office but find her door closed.

Mr. Underhill pauses his meet and greet with the students and catches my eyes. "Haven't seen her yet today."

"Oh. That's odd. She's usually here before me. Is she sick?"

"I don't know. We've got a call out to her, but she hasn't answered." He fist-bumps a third grader, and I wait while he finishes his routine.

"It's not really like her to be late."

"No. It's not."

"I could run over to her apartment and make sure she's okay," I offer.

He smiles, relieved. "Why don't you?"

MY FIST ECHOES OFF the wooden apartment door. "Carmen!" Her car is parked at the curb, so I know she is home. It's not like her to keep me waiting.

Her neighbor opens her door and peers out at me.

"Have you seen her?"

She shakes her head. "Have you called?"

"Of course I did. She didn't come to work. If she had answered her phone, I wouldn't—" I stop myself. It is not this old woman's fault. "I'm sorry. I'm just worried. It's not like her." I try the knob, but the door is locked. I pound again.

There is absolute silence from the other side of the door. The knot inside my stomach twists, and I envision her beaten unconscious because of the quest we've been on. I back up then ram against the door, slamming the wood with my shoulder the way policemen do in old movies.

"Oh, dear. Oh, dear." The woman frets behind me.

My voice is hoarse from calling out, and I spin, searching for something to pry against the door. "Call the police. Tell them something is wrong."

She hesitates, the creases on her face deepening, and I think she is going to tell me she doesn't want to get involved. But she turns into her apartment, and I see her lifting a black cordless phone. I rest against the door, still begging her to open the door but no longer crashing against the wood.

*Please let her be okay. I'll do whatever you want if she is just okay.* It's not a prayer to God. It's a negotiation with my own personal devil.

The police arrive, and with one swift kick, they gain access to the apartment.

"Stay here," one of the officers says, holding his hand out to me like he is halting traffic.

I call Mr. Underhill and relay what's happening as they clear the living room and the kitchen.

"Ms. Fuentes? This is the police. We are here for a wellness check. We have entered your apartment."

I peek inside as the officer at the door enters the living room. The other heads for the bedroom, and his voice stalls between wellness and check. He disappears inside, but his voice comes through loud and clear on his partner's radio. "Ten fifty-six. I need paramedics at 678 Tomlin Street, Apartment A."

I furrow my brow and whisper to Mr. Underhill, "What does ten fifty-six mean? In police code?"

"I don't know." He sounds hollowed out like me. I hear the clacking of the keyboard then the sharp intake of breath.

"What does it mean?" Words stall like the moment between a heartbeat, the silence between the squeeze and the release.

"Suicide."

I disconnect the phone and stand with my mouth open as my stomach plummets. I rush into the apartment and join the two officers in the bedroom.

I cannot make sense of the scene. She is in the closet, her bare feet pressed against the bottom of the door, holding it open. Her head lolls forward through the clothes, and her face is hidden by the sway of her hair. I cannot see her torso, but her hands dangle beneath the hem of a hanging shirt.

I shift, silent and unseen, and in the movement, I can see her face, mottled and puffy, and the cord wrapped around her neck. Her eyes are open, bulging. I wretch.

"Get her out of here, dammit. Set a perimeter!"

I am pushed, still hacking, from the apartment.

# Chapter 31

I don't remember driving home. I don't remember walking into my kitchen. I don't remember the light from the day being sucked out of the room, leaving me sitting in darkness.

When I hear a mechanical hum outside, I don't understand that it's the garage door opening until Chase turns the light on, and Jackson comes through the kitchen door.

The light blinds me. I drop my head into the shadow of my arms.

"What are you doing?" Chase asks.

I cannot speak. I shake my head. I may never speak again. I am only here because I had no place else to go.

"What's wrong with you?" He pats my head like I am a dog.

"You okay?" Jackson asks as he opens the refrigerator.

I need to get away from them. I can't breathe with them in the room, with all that light.

Chase sits in one of the chairs, leaning into me, pushing my hair back from my face. "What's wrong, babe?"

My breath hitches, and a sob breaks free. "She's dead." I mouth the words, but my voice won't come.

"I can't understand what you are saying. Jack, go get me a washcloth."

He mops my face and holds my hand, coaxing the impossible words. At some point, he lifts me from my seat and carries me to our bedroom. I melt into him because I have no bones left.

## Chapter 32

Through the night, I babble what I saw in Carmen's closet. Every time I open my eyes, he is there, holding me, whispering into my ear.

"She was always a little unstable, don't you think?" he asks in the darkest hour of the night.

"*No.*" I recoil. "I never... she wasn't—"

"Shhhhh."

I cry against his chest, sick with loss.

"I can take the day off if you need me to," he whispers when I wake and find that the dawn has come. I am tempted by his offer. The idea of moving forward into a reality where Carmen does not exist feels incomprehensible.

His arm comes into view as he settles the blanket over my shoulder. An angry scratch runs the length from his elbow to his wrist. Chase has a physical job and often arrives home with cuts and bruises, so it is a small normal in a world that no longer makes sense. I don't know why I feel the need to touch this one, but I run my finger over it.

"How did you do that?" It is the first time my voice has been more than a whisper, and it feels like a foreign thing in my mouth.

He turns his wrist over, making a fist so the scratch stands out, and blows out a long breath. "Who knows?" He folds the arm back around me and squeezes. "I'll take the day off."

"No. You don't have to do that. I'm okay." It's a lie. The moment Nick Underhill said the word "suicide," hollowness overtook all the places inside my body where organs used to be. I imagine my veins emptied out, my heart a silent vacuum. "I don't think I'm going back to the school."

"I don't blame you. That would be hard." He kisses my ear and asks me again if I am sure I don't want him to stay home. I assure him that I'll be fine.

Once he gets up to take a shower, I drag myself out of bed and down the steps to make coffee, to pack Jackson's lunch. There was something I was supposed to do today. Something important. *What was it?* The thought rattles in my head as I move on autopilot.

Chase says he'll drop Jackson at school even though I tell him that I can. He tells me to take the day.

I FORGET TO SHOWER. When he comes home, I am still sitting at the kitchen table with a cold cup of coffee in front of me.

"What did you do all day?" Irritation sparks on the edge of the concern in his voice.

I shake my head and push one hand through my dirty hair. He won't tolerate this long—the warning is stamped across his face. "I'm sorry." I look away from him, unable to hold his eyes. "I lost track of time. I'll do better."

"I hope so. You can't just disappear. You have a family. We count on you."

"I can fix dinner." I push away from the table, but he grabs my forearm before I can step away.

"Don't bother. I'll take him out. We've got Krav Maga anyway. Just clean yourself up. You stink."

# Chapter 33

It rains through the rest of November while snow blows on the mountain. Chase stays busy completing indoor projects the company has scheduled for the winter months—bathroom and kitchen remodels, painting. He starts work on the flip house he bought after the one on Broad Street sold.

I never went back to the school. I resigned in an email, which Mr. Underhill responded to with kind words and sympathy. He knew how much she meant to me, had seen our friendship firsthand.

Jackson's basketball season is in full swing, and Chase and I attend every game. Jackson is not a starter, but he almost always plays, and I am proud of his efforts. My body goes through the motions of living while the small woman inside of me cowers in a dark hole, barely able to see out.

Carmen is dead.

Carmen is dead.

Carmen is dead.

The knowledge is in every breath, every single heartbeat.

On Thanksgiving, we arrive at Chase's foreman's house to celebrate with others who don't have plans. We hosted last year. I bring pies and a green bean salad, which I make more for myself than anybody else. Chase brings a bottle of MacCallum's Scotch.

"Wow. You look great," Melanie says when I deliver my pies to her in the kitchen.

"Thank you." I smile and hope the cracks in my façade are not visible. It is important to Chase that I "hold it together" today. He doesn't want his team to know that I've "cracked."

"You're so skinny. Are you dieting? What are you doing?"

Now I understand her comment. It's the narrowness of my hips. The fact that I had to buy a new belt because mine had grown too long. Melanie is plump, and on her refrigerator is a magnet that says, "Nothing tastes as good as skinny feels."

"I don't know. I think I just lost interest in food." It is the truth, but I smile to soften it.

"I wish I could do that. I do fine until Halloween, and then I eat until January."

"You're beautiful the way you are. I don't think you should worry about it." I lean in, giving her a kiss on the cheek as if we are sisters or actual friends. "Where can I put these?"

She points to the buffet. I walk through the kitchen and into the formal dining room. Chase is standing with his back to me, his arm is raised and planted on the wall, and in the cage made by his body is his black-haired whore.

"Hi, Birdie," I call out to announce my presence in the room. Chase's arm falls, and he turns as Birdie slips off the wall and comes to take one of the pies. If I cared, I would be appalled.

"How are you doing?" There is genuine concern in her voice, and my eyes well with the surprise of it.

"I'm good." I manage, but my voice is in revolt, and I must turn away to keep from blubbering and find my smile. "I'm good. How are you?"

I set the pie down next to the one she has placed for me and proceed to remove the foil. It takes me a moment to look at her, but when I finally turn, I see that Chase has left and we are alone in the dining room.

She takes my hands in hers. "I know what it's like to lose somebody. If you ever need to talk..."

I pull one hand free to press against the bridge of my nose. "I appreciate that. Really, I do. But I'm fine."

"I lost my brother when I was six. I've never really gotten over it." She releases my other hand and turns to organize the buffet of desserts.

"What was his name?" I have to hear her say it.

"Mike. Mikey Dietz." She says the name like it is on a banner or in lights.

"I knew him. We graduated high school together." I'm shocked by my own words and bite the inside of my lip, feeling the threat of crossing lines, of telling her everything I think I know about the night her brother died. I almost feel alive.

"What was he like?" she asks, and I wonder what she remembers of him. She probably remembers the shock of him being dead more than the boy he was.

"We weren't friends, you know. I only went to Drake for a year, but I remember seeing him around." *Chase might remember him better than me.* The words echo in my head, reverberating. For a moment, I am afraid I have said them aloud, but she is still looking at me with some expectation.

"Well, if you ever need to talk, this is my number." She fishes in her pocket and comes out with a business card.

*Birdie Dietz, Martial Arts Academy, Instructor.*

"Instructor?" I whisper.

She looks embarrassed. Funny how she feels shy about her title but is comfortable facing me after sneaking around with my husband. Chase must've told her something awful about us—about me—that makes her feel like it is okay, that I don't deserve the decency of a husband who doesn't cheat. We stand for an awkward moment before she says again that I can call her anytime.

"I appreciate that. How did you, um, get through it?" I ask, feeling the catch on the words, the danger of having this conversation.

"We had a really good therapist. And I started martial arts so I would always be able to defend myself."

The doorbell rings, and the last of the guests filter in, chatter filling the space around us.

"Huh. Maybe I should try that."

"It saved my life."

I am not sure if she means therapy or martial arts. I make my excuses, find Melanie's bathroom, then reach for all the shattered pieces of my soul to pull them into place.

When I come out, Birdie is standing in the kitchen with Melanie. Chase is in the doorway and doesn't see me because he only has eyes for the black-haired girl. The expression on his face is forlorn, tormented, and I don't know what it means.

*Is he in love with her? Sincerely? Is this more than a fling?*

He looks up and catches me watching him. A flicker of confusion crosses his face but is replaced with a mask of arrogance. He winks at me and turns into the living room, where the men are lounging. I stay in the kitchen, sitting at the table next to Birdie after Melanie has assured me there is nothing I can do to help before dinner.

BIRDIE IS THE FIRST to leave. Chase offers to walk her to her car, but she declines. I wonder if the others see it and how many of them know. Chase takes us home not long after, pulling Jackson away from the Xbox and his friends in the basement.

Chase is crackling with frustration. "You and Birdie seemed to hit it off, didn't you?"

Jackson is in the backseat with his earbuds in, so I doubt he is listening.

"Yeah. She's a nice girl. I see why you like her."

"What does *that* mean?"

"You let her do payroll," I say, diffusing the heat. "She seems like a nice kid."

"Yeah. She is. What did you guys talk about?" He's still agitated, but I don't care.

"Her brother," I say, looking out the window, leaning my head against the cold glass.

"What about him?"

"Just that he died. She must know about... you know. Said if I ever needed to talk..." I let the offer complete itself and close my eyes.

The energy still radiates from him, and I keep motionless to not add to it. He will not hit me with Jackson home. Today will not be the next beatdown. I try to remember why I cared. I had worried once that he might beat something important out of me that made me who I was, but I can't recall what that thing was.

# Chapter 34

The week after Thanksgiving brings the snow from the mountain and covers the streets of the lowlands. I try to pull myself out of the hole inside by cleaning the house, cooking meals, and keeping off of Chase's radar. He always gives the crew the week after Thanksgiving off, so he is working solo on the flip house. He's been in a foul mood since the party, and even Jackson is keeping his distance, which is easy enough because he has basketball camp. On Tuesday, Chase is gone early, so it's up to me to drop Jackson at the gym.

I don't hear from Chase for the rest of the morning. I'm already late putting up the Christmas decorations, and I begin the cheerless task of dragging the boxes up from the basement.

A dark, opaque cloud has enveloped me, so I set the alarm on my phone. I have planned to visit Carmen's parents at one, and I don't want to forget. They have cleared out Carmen's apartment and said they have something for me. I assume it's my yearbook with my name imprinted on the cover. I should have visited before, but I'm barely making it through the days. I saw their grief at the funeral. I don't know that I can bear it in a social visit.

I set the tree base then begin the tedious process of inserting the individual limbs into the stand. We meant to pick up a new one after the season last year, one with the lights already strewn, but it didn't happen. My body moves on autopilot while my mind slides into numbness. I stop thinking, fitting the wire into the stand, matching the colors for the rows.

At eleven, my alarm pings, and I head out of the neighborhood to pick up burgers at Lamont's on Vine Street for Chase. The sun bounces off the snow, and I squint against the brightness. The drive-through line is wrapped around the building, but the lethargy overwhelms me, and I sit idling in my car, inching forward instead of simply going in.

I message Chase. *Is anybody helping? Do they want something?*

*No.* The curt response is typical of our texts these days.

My phone buzzes again. *Nice to see you remembered your phone.*

I can almost see the look on his face as he typed the words. Almost every conflict we have had in the past two months is about my phone. I've left it somewhere, forgot to charge it, or don't respond to his texts or phone calls. I don't mean to annoy him, but I set it down and forget it. Sometimes, I don't see texts until hours after he sent them, and by then, a response just makes him angrier. Strange how I used to be tethered to it. I always knew where it was.

I reach the speaker box and place my order. I inch toward the window and finally accept the bag of food from the young man. I pull forward then pause, digging into the bag to see that it contains everything Chase needs. There is no sauce. I must've forgotten to ask. I could go without it, but then the effort of getting it would have been wasted because Chase would be dissatisfied.

I park and push myself out of the car. It's not a big deal, but the weight of my legs trudging across the parking lot exhausts me, and pulling the door open makes me want to collapse in a heap on the ground. I reach the condiment island and select a variety of sauces to give Chase options.

"Ms. Stone." The name is on the air for several seconds before I register someone is speaking to me. I turn to see a fully bearded Nick Underhill standing from his table to greet me.

The sight of him sends shame coursing through me. I never did go back to the school, just folded like a bad hand in poker. "Mr. Underhill, I—"

"Nick. Please."

"Nick."

"It's good to see you. How are you?" He holds my eyes with his, and I see him searching through the clutter to see if I am still inside.

I smile quickly and look away. "I-I should have come by the school, made sure you had the library covered. I'm so sorry about that." I crinkle my nose as if I can smell my failure, but I can't bring myself to put on a front with him.

"Oh, it was fine. I totally understand. I've wanted to come by your house to see that you were okay but wasn't sure if that would be... acceptable." His brows furrow, and I wonder how much Carmen told him about me. About Chase.

"That's kind." I breeze past the suggestion that a visit would have caused conflict for me. I can only imagine the beatdown that would have been inspired by this handsome man stopping by the house for my sake.

We are stalled, suddenly strangers without any remaining connection. "Looks like you are heading somewhere," Nick says. "I won't keep you. But it was really good to see you. If you ever decide you want to come back, we'll always have a place for you."

"Really?" A single tear breaches my lashes and courses down my face.

He gives my shoulders a gentle squeeze. "Yes, and even if it's not Eastside, you can count on me for a letter of reference."

"That's very kind of you. Maybe next year."

He nods. "Maybe. The kids all miss you. Come by sometime. They'd love to see you."

"I'll do that."

He walks me to the door and holds it open for me as if he senses I'll never set foot in Eastside again. "Take care of yourself."

"You too. It was great to see you."

When I get back in my car, a small point of light is glowing in the darkness of my soul. The shame about the way I quit is stilled, its screaming face silenced. In its place is a bridge—a connection.

CHASE'S TRUCK SITS in the shelter of the open garage, and I park in the ruts on the street, taking in the neighborhood and the general atmosphere of decay. It is a beautiful day, and the sheen on the snow suggests a coming thaw. The wind that blew snow down from the mountain has finally relented, and for the first time in a week, the sky is a brilliant, vivid blue. I take my time, standing in the sunshine, looking around at the houses planted down the street.

The neighborhood looks like it was new in the 1980s. I expect the older population is beginning to die off or be moved into assisted living facilities. Lots of these homes are hitting the market. Three doors down on the left is a house that has already been updated, and a young man is on a ladder, stringing lights while his two kids roll the base for a snowman. It looks like a postcard. I wouldn't have seen the potential in the neighborhood, but Chase did. He's always good at seeing the big picture.

I step in the footprints already pressed into the snow and enter the house through the garage. Chase is midswing with a sledgehammer, bringing down the cabinets in the kitchen, and it's like an explosion. I am hyper-focused on his movements, trying to gauge his mood. *Should I just leave the food and go?*

Finally, I cross the threshold, but my foot collides with a cardboard box. I stumble, nearly losing the bag of food. Catching myself on the corner of the box, I dent it where the flap is folded under its partner. I right myself, my heart racing at the near catastrophe. I wait for my heart to steady before calling out.

"What?" he demands, turning toward me.

"I, uh..." The rage doesn't make sense, and for a split second, I think he is going to come at me. My knees feel liquid. Even though it's impossible, I can't help but wonder if he knows I ran into Nick Underhill and assumes I was flirting, or worse, having an affair. "I brought you lunch."

The mottled expression clears, and he blinks. "Oh, great. That's great. Thanks. What did you get?"

"Lamont's."

"Good call." He sets down the sledgehammer and heads toward me. When I hand over the bag, he looks up at me. "You didn't get anything?"

"No. My stomach's off. I'm heading over to see Carmen's folks. I don't think I can eat."

"You gotta get past that shit."

I nod slowly. "I just owe them a visit." Chase's tolerance for my grief reached its limit weeks ago. "Can I look around?"

He shrugs.

Old carpet has been pulled up, revealing scarred and damaged hardwood beneath. *That's a treasure.* Two walls have been knocked out to create a more open floor plan between the kitchen and the living room. I make my way up the steps and into the bedrooms, imagining how the space will transform with gleaming floors and light converging from the windows.

When I come down, I hear his voice, low and intense, and my stomach flutters. We are getting close, I know, to that next beatdown. He is frustrated by my lethargy, annoyed by my sadness. But now his irritation is directed at the person on the other end of the phone.

"Fine. Fine. Whatever you need to do. I think you are making a huge mistake." He pauses. "Either you're on my team, or you're not." It sounds like the severing of ties.

I've heard that before. Chase has used that exact phrase on me whenever I've balked or questioned him. I wonder who is stepping outside of his bubble now.

I've stalled on the steps, trying to decide if I can get out the front door without him hearing me if I need to.

"Delilah!"

I jump then rush down the rest of the stairs and around the wall.

He's in the demolished kitchen, hunched over the crumpled food bag, glaring at his burger. "You know who that was?"

"On the phone?" I shake my head, unable to read him.

"That was Birdie."

I nod, unsure. "How is she?"

"I don't know, Delilah. You tell me."

I take a single step toward the door. "I wouldn't know." *She's your girlfriend.* I am tempted to spit the words, to let him know that I know, but I don't dare.

"What the fuck did you say to her at Thanksgiving?" He takes a bite of his burger and chews with a vengeance, the muscles of his jaws working, working, working.

"I didn't say anything to her. She approached me. Told me to call her if I wanted to talk about Carmen."

"What does she know about Carmen?" He drops the half-eaten burger and steps toward me, and I look for my escape route.

"Nothing! She just said that she knew something about losing people and that her brother died when she was little. That's all. She said I could call her if I needed to talk. Jesus, Chase, stop. You're scaring me."

"You said something—I fucking know you did. You are never on my team. Sneaky bitch. You're always working against me."

"Oh my God, that is not true!" Even if he is right, I didn't do anything to mess up what he and Birdie had going. "What in the world did she say I said to her?"

"Nothing, but she just quit!" He throws up his hands, pacing. "Says she's taking a job with a contractor out of Drake."

Through the large plate-glass window, I notice the man I saw stringing lights earlier approach the house, probably drawn by our raised voices.

Chase follows the direction of my eyes, and when I look back at him, he is staring with venom at the man. His anger restrained, he turns away from the window and stomps into the kitchen. His hand slides down the shaft of the sledgehammer then brings it down once on the cabinet with full force.

"Maybe you can offer her a raise. If she just needs more money—"

"You better go." He glowers at me. "Don't want to be late for your date."

I head out the door but linger on the step. From the porch, I can still see the father staring from his yard. "I'm sorry about Birdie. It's a shame."

"Yes. It's a shame." He sneers, pushing his hand up through his hair.

Blazing a new trail through the snow, I don't look up to see if Chase or the man are watching.

"I'll see you at home!" I call out for the man's sake before I duck into my car as if I'm unconcerned about Chase and his anger. My heart hammers. My blood jolts through my veins, and for a second, I think I may be alive.

# Chapter 35

By the time I reach the Fuentes' house, my heart rate has sunk to its barely beating state, and the flare of adrenaline that Chase's outburst caused is only an unsettling memory. Fatigue from the drive and the effort of carrying the Christmas decor from the basement weighs on me. Only the chance encounter with Nick Underhill at Lamont's and that small dissolution of guilt give me strength to go forward.

I park in front of the Fuentes' house and sit for a long minute, garnering the energy to push myself out of the car. Resting my forehead on the steering wheel, I consider a short nap, but I have put this meeting off longer than I should have. *I'm going to melt when I see them.*

When Carmen died, I had to wonder if her parents knew something that I missed. She'd never opened up to me about her mental health problems. Maybe I was so wrapped up in my own drama that she didn't think she could, and I never looked for warning signs. Clearly, she put a lot of thought into her death to have just the right length of rope. My thoughts spiral as I picture the taut rope, her feet against the closet door, and I must pull myself out of the car and the cyclone to keep from sliding into the depths. I couldn't do anything for Carmen back then. The least I can do is check on her parents.

No tracks lead from the driveway toward the house, so I force my feet into the virgin snow. Carmen's dad, Martin, steps out of the garage, wiping his hand on an oil-stained rag.

"Mr. Fuentes?" I call, waving as I make my way.

"What a nice surprise. Joan know you're stopping by?"

"Yes. We've been texting."

"Well, nice to see you. How's Jackson?"

"He's good. In high school now." I put my hand up to illustrate how tall he has gotten. "How are you?" Sudden tears erupt, and I look away to push them down. They are always right there, just on the edge.

"Getting by." The hitch in his voice suggests that he is walking on the same edge. He drapes an arm over my shoulder, and we walk together into the house.

"Joan, we have a visitor."

The house is fragrant with a pot roast simmering in a Crock-Pot. The kitchen is clean and crisp, all whites and yellows, old-fashioned, much like the kitchen Chase is demolishing.

"What are you hollering about?" Joan asks, coming from the living room. "Oh, Delilah." She smiles, and I see Carmen in the way her lips part. I never noticed that before.

"I should have come sooner. I'm so sorry." More tears spring, and we hug.

"It's been such a shock." She gives me an extra squeeze before she lets go. I nod, trying to get control. When we step back, I see that her face is as soppy as mine.

"How's Jackson?"

Focusing on the living brings us to even footing. We sit at the kitchen table, and I tell them about Jackson's basketball team and how Chase has started a new flip project. Their oldest son, Ramone, has just had his second daughter.

"Oh, congratulations."

"They named her Carmella—that's what he used to call Carmen when they were kids."

My face crumples, and I pull my hand up to cover my eyes. We were freshmen in college when he was a senior, and I remember him calling out to her with that pet name. "I'm still in such shock over everything," I whisper when I can speak again. "I never would have imagined this."

Joan pats my hand. "She never said anything about being depressed to you?"

"No. Never."

They exchange a worried look. "Us either."

We sit in silence for a long minute. Carmen must've kept her pain so bundled up that none of us even knew she was sad. The fresh pain in her parents' eyes tell me they must be feeling the same guilt as me.

"You said you, uh, have some things of mine, from her apartment?"

"I'll go get it." Joan gets up from the table.

I am ashamed that it is this that has finally brought me to visit them—my high school yearbook and all the research we bundled together about Michael Dietz. It's insane that we thought it mattered. She was in pain, and I was so self-absorbed that all I could think about was me and my ridiculous plan to get rid of my husband.

Joan returns with a single envelope.

"What's this?"

"We had her mail forwarded, and this came after the funeral."

I take the envelope and understand. It is from Dorrell, the prison that houses Dabney Holt. It is addressed to me, and I expect they have a matching one with her name on it. I shake my head and fold the envelope to put it into my purse. "I hate to ask, but there was a yearbook. I should probably get that too."

Joan frowns at her husband. "I don't remember a yearbook, do you?"

Martin shrugs.

The concern on my face must be obvious because Joan offers to help me look through the boxes. She leads me down the hall and up the stairs to what had been Carmen's childhood room. Joan has turned it into a sewing room, but Carmen's bed is still along one wall, now overflowing with boxes from her apartment. There are stacks on the floor as well. Joan and I unearth one labeled BOOKS.

Sure enough, the yearbook is not there. I scan the other boxes. "Maybe it was with her papers. We were doing research for a project about a boy we graduated high school with."

"We didn't find any papers. We found her old journals but nothing that looked like research."

"That's odd. She kept it in the bottom drawer of her desk, I think." I remember her slipping the copies I had brought from the newspaper into that drawer.

"There wasn't anything in her desk."

"*Nothing*?"

Joan shakes her head.

"That's odd."

"You can look through all of this. I don't know what I'm going to do with it." Tears brim in her eyes, and I fear I have overstayed my welcome.

"Would you mind? I feel terrible asking, but I just feel like I should finish the project." I reach out and touch her arm. She nods and tells me to go right ahead.

I search every box, but not a single item pertaining to Michael Dietz or Dabney Holt surfaces. My yearbook might as well have never existed.

# Chapter 36

By the time I reach the house, I almost think I imagined all the notes and research we had compiled about Michael Dietz and Dabney Holt. Maybe Carmen took them into the school. Maybe she gave them to the retired Aldrich detective she was supposed to meet that Friday—something I'd forgotten about in the wake of the tragedy. I picture the collection sitting in the trunk of her car and feel somewhat better. Of course she would have put everything together in preparation for her meeting with Young.

My uneasiness settles with the explanation, and I wonder where her car is now. My mind rolls through her taking the research, packed into a box or a crate, to the car. The image sputters as she turns to go back up to her apartment.

If she planned to kill herself Thursday, she wouldn't have prepared for a Friday meeting. It's a loose end, and I can't figure out how it ties together. I risk a quick internet search for Detective Scott Young's phone number and find that he does private investigation in retirement. The photograph on his website shows a solid man in his late fifties with close-cropped salt-and-pepper hair.

I should wait to call him from my burner phone, but I've already done the search, and if Chase is watching, it's too late. I'm not even sure I care.

"Scott Young Agency. This is Scott." His deep baritone voice has the rasp of a smoker, the low register rattling against his vocal cords.

"Mr. Young, I'm a friend of Carmen Fuentes. She was researching an old case you had worked."

"Yes." He doesn't give anything away.

"You were scheduled to meet with her a couple of weeks ago. I'm wondering if she may have brought anything to your office."

"Carmen Fuentes..." The name rolls off his tongue, and I imagine him looking through his schedule to place it. "She never showed."

"No. She died that week. I was wondering if she brought anything to you before your meeting. I can't find her research, so I was just following up."

"Sorry, she didn't bring anything to me. I'm afraid I can't help you."

ON THURSDAY, AFTER I have finally finished decorating the house, I carry the empty tubs and boxes down the basement steps and stack them along the studded wall. When I turn around, I notice a box out of place. It sits on the floor between the man-shaped punching bag and the arms of the Bowflex. Unlike the others, this box is unmarked, and the top is folded in on itself, not taped. I lift one flap and the others break free, revealing paperwork.

I cannot make sense of it until I shift the box toward the light. When the box tilts, some of the pile slides, exposing the gloss of a book. I reach in and withdraw it, my eyes lingering on the name—my name—embossed on the lower right side. It doesn't make sense.

Then it does.

I tripped over this box the day I went to the flip house. It has the exact crease in the flaps from when I used it to break my fall. Understanding bolts through me, staggering me like lightning. *Chase.* There is no other answer. He stole the yearbook and research from Carmen's apartment and stashed it at the flip house before bringing it here. Chase was in Carmen's apartment. He was there the night she died. My fingers dig into the yearbook cover. Carmen would never kill herself.

Relief washes over me. She wasn't depressed. I didn't miss the signs. Guilt rises like bile in its place. She is dead because of me. Because I was too big of a coward to just leave my husband.

*Did he drug her?* The details of the morning after I found her flood my mind. Him being so kind. The scratch running the length of his forearm. Carmen must've fought against him before he overpowered her.

The garage door begins to ratchet up, and I toss the yearbook into the box then slam the flaps shut. I reach the top of the stairs as the kitchen door creaks open, and Chase and Jackson shuffle in, home from Krav Maga. I shut the door to the basement as I slip out, pretending to admire the tree twinkling in the corner.

"Mom!" Jackson calls from somewhere inside the refrigerator. "What's for dinner?"

Pasting a smile on my face, I walk into the kitchen, careful not to look at Chase. "Let's order pizza. I'm pooped."

"You get everything up?" Chase fills his water bottle now that Jackson has given way at the fridge.

"I did." I wash my hands at the sink. "Just took the boxes back downstairs." I glance at him, but he is unconcerned, drinking.

I should have listened to Carmen and called the police when he followed me to her apartment that night. I should have documented my injuries and filed for sole custody of Jackson. Maybe then I could have gotten a restraining order. The litany of all my wrong choices is devastating. I know better now. If I survive the next beatdown, then I'll do what I should have done last summer.

# Chapter 37

The following Friday, Jackson's basketball team plays on Drake's court. Chase is finishing a project at work and tells me to go on without him. He'll meet me there. I don't want to go, but I pull on my Vikings sweatshirt and drag myself out of the house.

It is a packed gymnasium. The rivalry between Aldrich and Drake brings crowds. It was the same when I was in school. After paying my admission, I make my way to the visitors' bleachers and set my purse on the bench beside me to save a seat for my husband.

The first quarter is over before Chase arrives. I make room for him as he looks up at the scoreboard. The Drake team is up by ten already, leaving him irritated. "It's gonna be a slaughter."

"They might come back."

"Has Jack even played?"

"No, not yet."

The muscles in his jaw twitch, and he looks toward the bench to find Jackson.

"You want anything from the concession stand?"

"No."

"I think I'm going to get some popcorn. Okay?"

He shrugs, and I climb out of the bleachers and away from him. I don't want to be here. I don't want to hear the noise of the sneakers on the floor, the chaos of the crowd cheering. I don't want to sit next to Chase and pretend that I am okay. I am out of the gymnasium before the energy coming from Chase dissipates. It's overwhelming—like I'm trapped under a weighted blanket. Two days ago, I thought it was going to happen. I was all but braced for impact when Jackson came down the stairs from his room, and Chase's rage was diverted. He's still angry that I can't pull myself out of my funk and about Birdie leaving him. He still thinks I said something to her.

Once Jackson passed through the room, Chase leaned toward me, his index finger extended, almost touching my cheek. "You have a choice. You either live with what you got, or you don't." He spun, grabbed his keys, and left the house.

Chase was right. I had to live with what I had or not. I went to bed expecting him to show up somewhere in the night, but when I woke at three, he wasn't home. He came in as I was leaving to take Jackson to school, freshly showered and shaved.

"Where did you stay?" I asked, knowing the danger in questioning him, almost hoping his rage would stir so Jackson could witness the demon firsthand.

"At the flip house." He scrutinized me for a long second like he knew I wouldn't believe him. Like he thought I would come out and ask if he was with another woman. As if I cared.

But I know what he did to Carmen. That's the only thing that matters now.

I stand in line for the popcorn and dawdle until I hear the second-quarter buzzer, and the chaos of boys and sneakers erupts again.

My seat has been taken. Two men have shifted the other patron down the bench to make room. I hesitate. Chase is smiling, laughing at something the man has said. *Should I find another seat?* But once Chase catches sight of me, he nods me over.

"You remember Tom, don't you?" I shake the nearest man's hand, and when I look at his face, I can see the young man he was, thinned out and hollow. Not so different from now.

"Tom Lassiter." The name rolls off my tongue. "How are you?" Thank God I didn't make it to his name on the list of witnesses. I glance at Chase, and his eyes are intent on me.

"Just fine. Real good. Trying to get this old fart to retire so I can take over the business." Tom punches the other man's arm.

"You still got a lot to learn, Gumshoe," the older man says in a raspy voice. He turns, and I recognize him from the photo on Scott Young's website.

"I'm Scott." He rises, and the baritone voice confirms that it could be nobody else. The detective offers a calloused hand, and we shake.

"We all play softball together," Chase explains at my confused look. "This is my wife, Delilah."

"Good to meet you," Scott says.

"You too." I offer Chase the popcorn, but he shakes his head.

Tom clears his throat. "Well, look here. We've taken your seat. We'll go find our own."

They maneuver off the bench.

A twitch begins in my eyelid as it dawns on me how Carmen and I screwed up.

"All right, my friend," Tom says to Chase. "I guess we'll see you around."

"Not if I see you first."

They chuckle, and Tom pats my shoulder as they leave.

I settle again next to Chase, and he grabs a handful of popcorn. His mood is better, and when Jackson is put in the game, he calls out, "Let's go, Jack!"

My mind reels. "They look alike. Family?"

Chase looks at me, smiling, popcorn kernels in his teeth. "Oh yeah. Tom is Scott's nephew. Pretty much raised him. You didn't know that?"

I shake my head. "Why would I know that?"

"Went to school with him. You'd think you woulda known." He turns back to the game. "Not as smart as you thought you were." His words are nearly lost as Aldrich scores, and a cheer goes up in the crowd. I'm not even certain I've heard them. Chase pinches the bag of popcorn between his knees to clap.

I close my eyes and see the trap. My stomach flops. I never considered the possibility that Tom Lassiter worked with Scott Young, let alone how close they were. *We were so dumb.* I can just imagine the conversation in that office after Carmen made her appointment regarding the Dietz case. Tom knows about Dietz—I am certain. He was probably involved. He might've held Dietz down while Chase beat him. *Did Young not look for that last sample because he knew his nephew might be involved?*

I warned Carmen that Chase knew some of the police. We should've been more careful. Chase knows everybody. And if Scott Young and his nephew were in on Dabney Holt's framing and tipped Chase off, that would take the whole case to a different level. It's not just my husband who will go down if the truth about Michael Dietz comes out. I don't want to believe it.

Chase knows. *Why hasn't he killed me yet?* He arranged tonight. It was a reminder that I could either live with what I got or not.

Chase offers me the popcorn, but my stomach has soured. I shake my head, keeping my eyes on Jackson. Watching him is the only thing keeping me from coming apart at the seams.

It's only through Chase's good cheer that I know we've won when the final buzzer sounds. He joins the team on the court with other fathers, congratulating their sons and complimenting each other on their successes.

I can barely breathe.

# Chapter 38

I arrange to meet with Holt the following Thursday. At this point, it feels like there is no reason not to. Chase knows what we were looking into, that I am not on his team. It is just a matter of time before he kills me. I don't even care. I owe it to Carmen. I owe it to Desirey Holt. I owe it to the world to right the wrongs that my husband has committed. Besides, Chase doesn't have connections in Dorrell, so maybe this one thing will be off his radar.

I build an alibi for the outing, saying that I will be out Christmas shopping. I make a big production of asking for lists, knowing that neither he nor Jackson will provide them. I'll have to do my shopping without their input, the same every year. I drive to the mall in time for it to open and send one last text to Chase.

*Let the shopping commence!*

*Have fun.*

My iPhone in hand, I make my way through the crowds to Dillard's. Inside, I power the phone down then slide it under a stack of jeans on the lowest shelf in the big-and-tall section. I can't have Chase checking my location today.

I drive down State Road 37 toward Dorrell, filling the car with one-sided conversation, repeating phrases and questions I want to ask. A conversation that has my stomach churning and my mind spinning.

I scan the mirrors, looking for Chase on my tail as the car hurtles through traffic toward a man that the world thinks is a murderer. *Focus.*

When my speed approaches sixty, a small shimmy begins in the front end, and I'm forced to slow down. I reach for my phone to ask

Chase about it but then remember my mission and that my phone is sheltering under jeans at Dillard's.

My notebook and tape recorder rest on the seat beside me, and I run through the series of questions again. I wish I had my senior yearbook. It would be better to let him pick Chase out the way Renae had than to offer his name and ask directly if he was at the party.

If I can get Dabney Holt to put in the call about Chase, then maybe he won't have the chance to kill me.

We are on the edge, and if he finds out about today, it will happen sooner rather than later. The tension has mounted since Carmen died—before then, probably, but that feels like a different life. It's about Birdie too. Maybe she got tired of being the other woman, not understanding that it was better than being me.

"Probably," I say aloud. The admission sounds like a deflated balloon, falling limp from my lips. "Everybody gets to move on except for me," I whisper in a made-up rhythm to a child's clapping game.

I stalled after Carmen died. I cannot reconcile her death, her murder. I push her out of my mind and focus on the road, letting the silence envelop me like armor. The car hums and rolls, and the shimmy in the front end becomes more pronounced.

"Tigers don't change their stripes." I repeat the words Carmen said when I'd told her I was going back to Chase again.

A long minute stretches into two, and I wallow, feeling sorry for my sad, broken life. "Why am I doing this? It feels so dangerous."

"We're just talking to him," Carmen's voice says next to me. "Just finding out what he remembers about that night. We'll know if he's telling the truth."

"Then what?" I look over at the passenger seat, irritated that she hasn't kept up with the moving pieces. *Chase knows. We know. Everybody fucking knows what really happened to Michael Dietz, and it doesn't matter.* I am baffled to find the seat empty.

Maybe Chase is right. Maybe I have cracked, rolling through a conversation as if Carmen is here talking to me. I forgot or was unaware that all the words were coming from my lips. Carmen is dead.

I bite down, stemming the flood of words. But I'm unable to slow the conversation in my head. If he seems like a good guy, or if he can place Chase at the party that night, then I'll turn it over to the police. *'Cause that worked out really well.*

Maybe I was jumping to conclusions. But I didn't know why Tom, who would have known about Carmen's meeting with Young, would have mentioned it to Chase. He would have called him if he'd known that Chase killed Dietz. He would have called him if they had covered it up together. I should turn the car around. I wondered if Young was involved.

At the game, Tom and Scott had seemed to be there as a warning, but they could've just bumped into Chase and stopped to visit. Maybe Tom wasn't involved and had only mentioned the Dietz case to Chase in passing. They would have both remembered the Dietz murder.

I feel like I'm grasping at straws. There was nothing that would have tied Chase to Carmen's interest in Michael Dietz when she called Young. She didn't tip her hand. She would have used the cover story. It would have seemed legit. If he googled Cheryl Buxton, he would have found her books and known this would be in her wheelhouse. My head aches trying to make sense of it.

But whether their meeting at the game was planned or a coincidence, it told me what I needed to know. The three men were close. One casual comment was all it would have taken to clue Chase in on Carmen's planned meeting.

I know it in my gut what Chase has done. He might have killed her to keep her from talking to Young. I don't know what Chase wouldn't do to get away with murder. But the fact is I don't have anything except my suspicions and the box of research that I don't dare touch again.

"I won't know until I talk to Dabney Holt." That's all there is to it.

The silence returns to the vehicle, but my mind rages on. *I could just keep driving. I could just drive as far as I could go and then walk away from my life.*

*I can't leave my son.*

*Dammit.*

He called me an "alibi." That means something. I flip the signal to exit the interstate. *Why would he say that?*

*Because he was pissed and trying to make you feel worthless.*

*True.* I look in the mirror with narrowed eyes but say nothing. He may kill me—he probably will—but I'm going to take him down with me. I'm on the cusp of exposing him.

*I'm not worthless. I'm not stupid. I may have been a coward, but that ends today.*

# Chapter 39

After a long minute sitting in my car, I steel my determination and head for the prison, feeling the weight of the ride in every limb. My hips have gotten so narrow that my jeans hang only by the constraint of my belt, and the fabric bunches at my ankles. I walk up to the front entrance, and the guards allow me through the first set of gates. I show my identification again at the second gate, and the guard asks, "Who are you visiting?"

"Dabney Holt." My voice breaks on the name, and the guard makes a note in the computer then releases the electric lock for me.

No personal items are allowed in the visiting hall, and I must leave my purse, the notebook, and the recorder in a locker. I had hoped they would at least let me take the recorder, but they do not bend the rules, and I am too intimidated to suggest it.

"There is no touching the inmates. Keep your mouth fully visible at all times. There are vending machines, and you are allowed to take up to thirty-three dollars inside in a clear Ziplock bag. Coins and singles only." I haven't brought cash for a vending machine and realize that I should have. Something from the vending machine would probably feel like a real treat to Dabney Holt.

After I've agreed to the terms, I am shown into a visiting room, and another guard points for me to sit.

Eventually, the door at the other end of the hall opens, and a guard enters. A man stoops behind him to come through. I knew Dabney Holt was a big guy from the photo on *Just InJustice's* website, but it hardly captured the magnitude of him. His wrists are cuffed, forcing his hands to hang in front of his crotch. Once he's clear of the door, he straightens to his full height. His pate is shining and bald, and though his face is clean-shaven, he looks about as disreputable as a man can. He doesn't walk to the table—he saunters, taking his time, his hips and cuffed hands leading the procession of his body. This is a man who looks fully capable of bludgeoning another man to death. I understand why he was a target.

When he finally reaches the table, I stand and hold out my hand. "I'm Delilah Stone. It's nice to meet you. I'm interested in your story."

He looks at my proffered hand like I've offered a stinking fish, and I remember the instruction not to touch the inmates.

"Right. Sorry." I tuck my hand away, blushing.

He slumps down on the bench on the other side of the table. "You writing a book?"

A small, deprecating laugh escapes me. As if I would ever be capable of such a thing. "No. Not me. I explained that in my letter. Did you get it?"

He shrugs, and I have a hard time not gawking at his hulking frame.

"I'm part of the advance team for Cheryl Buxton. We're looking at several possibilities, but the story is, ah... it's in development." He doesn't seem to recognize Cheryl Buxton's name, so I add, "She wrote *The Raven's Song*. She's got a few others, but that's her most famous one."

"I don't read much." Desirey had told me as much.

"Nobody does anymore."

"My mother was a reader. She probably read that. She read 'bout everything."

"My mother was a big reader too." I smile, and the tension eases in my back. He had come through the door looking like a bonified killer, but now I see the person Desirey described. A little slow, maybe. Child-like. I wouldn't have pegged him as a man who would rescue bunnies, but hearing him speak makes it more plausible.

Time stretches, and an awkward silence envelops us. "Well, tell your mother to keep reading. Cheryl will send her a signed copy when she finishes."

"Wish she could. Mom passed."

"Oh, I'm sorry to hear that." I can't remember if Desirey mentioned that. "I guess we tend to think our mothers will live forever."

He settles his arms across the table. His eyes drop to his bound hands, and the wall between us rebuilds. When he again looks at me, he is the intimidating man that stooped through the door. "So, what you wanna know?"

"I'm interested in the Michael Dietz murder," I say as if he needs clarification on which of his deeds I am here to discuss.

"Yep."

"Why'd you do it?" The words feel risky tripping over my lips, like little demons set free into the world. I need to hear it from him.

He furrows his brow, all remnants of the simpleton gone. "I *didn't*."

"Doesn't everybody say that?" My lips quirk into a tentative smile in an effort to remove any judgement from my words. I wish Carmen was here with me. She would know how to talk to him. I can't just tell him I think my husband did it if there is any chance that I am wrong.

"Yep, but I really didn't. I done other things, but I didn't kill that boy."

"Do you have any idea who might have? Did you even know Michael Dietz?"

"Yeah. Everybody knew Dietz."

I am jarred. That's exactly what Chase said years ago. That puts Chase and this mammoth of a man in the same circle.

"What was he like?"

"I don't know. I mean, I scored some stuff from him. It wasn't like we hung out, though."

"So you weren't friends?"

"We weren't *not* friends." His eyes move from me to his hands.

"Who do you think killed him?"

Holt leans back in his seat, drawing his hands in, the cuffs scrapping over the Formica surface of the table. He looks up as if trying to pull a name from the fluorescent overheads. "I don't know. My sister has a list of everybody who was at that party. You should talk to her. She probably knows more about it than me."

"I've spoken with her. I have the list. She's pretty certain you didn't do this."

"'Cause I didn't," he says, cocky, confident.

"Tell me about that night?"

"It was nothing special. School was fixing to let out. We were just all *done,* you know? Ready for summer. Everybody had steam."

"You were a student?" I hadn't read that in any of the research.

"No, man, not me. I was working at the Jiffy Lube, but college was about done, and most folks was about to be heading out of town, back to where they came from."

"It felt like change?" I offer, and he nods and shrugs at the same time. "What time did you arrive at the party?"

"Around seven. Dietz was already there and set up like he did every Friday night, in that back room. His office, see? It was the only time you could get to him. The rest of the week, he was under the radar. Know what I mean?"

"He was dealing drugs?" I whisper, eyeing the guard by the door.

"Ain't that what I just said?" Now he looks at me like I'm the slow one.

I know about the drug-deal-gone-bad theories. Mindy mentioned that Chase and Dietz were in business together. Chase dealt in Drake and Dietz in Aldrich. Maybe that was how Dietz stayed "under the radar."

*But if they didn't like being seen together, why was Chase there?* I haven't worked up to that yet. "What were you going to get?" I ask instead.

"Man, I had already done got. That's why I'd gone back to him—I was, like, trippiiiiing and shiiiiit." He draws the words out, stretching them into unfathomable lengths. "And I needed Dietz to fix my head, get it? Like, I needed the *antidote*."

Suddenly, he sits up then leans across the table, his voice low and intense. "I walked into that room, and he was lying there on the floor, all busted up and broke. Broken like nothing I had ever seen before, and I thought I had done gone off the deep end. Thought it was all part of the trip, *man*." His hands draw up to his eyes as if blocking the sight. They fall again to the table, banging against the surface and making me jump. "I got the PTSD from that shit, man. I still see it sometimes, all vivid and shit. Real living color, you know?"

I nod but offer no words.

"So, like, there had been a ton of people at that party—like, a fucking *lot*—and yeah, I had been in there, and yeah, that was my damn hat that he was lying on, but that don't mean that I killed him. Man, I liked Dietz. He had always been straight with me. He was *reeeal*. He *got* it."

"How do you think his body ended up on your hat?"

"Well, like, he was also on a jacket, and that wasn't mine. It was a coat room. That's where everybody threw their shit."

"Why do you think the police targeted you?"

A wry compression of his lips and a widening of his eyes answers the question. "Have you seen me?"

"You think they targeted you because you're a big guy?"

"Yeeeah."

"I read the police report. It said that you discovered the body and went back out to party. It said you didn't 'raise the alarm.'"

"No, that ain't right. Man, I went out and started telling *everybody* that somebody ought to check on Mikey. I totally thought I was just tripping and having a bad ride. I needed a fucking *antidote*. I thought it was some part of the shit in my head, like the snakes and the water raining everywhere but on me." He never once looks away, and I lean in, sensing the truth of his words. "That's why the cops put a target on me, man. 'Cause I *told* people. If I'd have just kept my mouth shut and walked away, they'd still be looking for the unknown specimen."

"Tell me about that—'the unknown specimen.'" I know it had to be Chase. Mindy placed him at the crime scene, but I want to know if Dabney has a theory.

"There was a lot of DNA in that room, and they identified and *spoke* with every single person belonging to that DNA except for one duuude."

The last word lasts forever, and I shift in my seat, waiting for it to end. Nothing he has said has made him sound dim, but his manner of speaking makes him sound like an idiot.

"Why didn't they talk to him?" My stomach churns, and I fold my hands in my lap to keep them still.

"Because they *couldn't.* They never found him."

"And they already had you, so they didn't look very hard," I whisper.

"Yeeeah." Holt sounds like a man who has walked many miles without sustenance and finally sees a juicy orange. But it's a mirage—there is no book in the works, and I've been too big of a coward to offer my husband up to the police.

I feel the weight of the circumstances that landed Dabney Holt in prison. I believe *Just InJustice* had it right. The police rushed it for closure. Chase didn't have leverage with the cops back then. Tom Lassiter would have, though. He would have protected Chase. Tom would have discouraged his uncle "who nearly raised him" from looking at his best friend.

*Why did he need me, then, if Tom had that kind of pull?* I was his ticket out of town. That was why he approached me that night and wanted me again.

Blood rushes under my skin as I remember the terror I felt in the moments when Chase knocked me to the floor and towered above me. When the rage hit, he grew, morphed into a giant creature with bulging muscles and ripping hands. The same demon who stole Carmen from me. *What kind of guy would protect someone like that?*

*A guy who was in on it.* I'm seeing demons in every shadow and can't tell if I'm getting paranoid or if the connections are logical.

I clear my throat. "Your family has been very vocal about your innocence."

"Yeah. They *know* I would'na ever been able to do something like this. My parents even put up the reward. Not that it has mattered."

"How much was the reward?"

"Fifty thou. They've mortgaged their home for it."

"That's a lot of money."

"Yep. It's set up in a trust. Nobody's touched it."

With that much money, I could rebalance myself. I could start over.

"What was the murder weapon?" I ask, shifting gears to see if I can throw his innocent man routine.

"It was never recovered, but Mikey had this bat that he carried around with him. Nobody ever saw it again after that. I'd bet it was what done him in."

"Can you tell me about the bat?"

He looks at me as if I am stupid. "It was just a fuckin' bat. What is there to tell? It was yay long. Made of wood."

"Anything that could identify it as his bat?" I press on.

Holt sits back a moment. "Yeah. He had his initials carved in the handle."

"The knob?"

He nods, and I lean back in my seat, wondering how much more I dare say. "The bat isn't mentioned in any of the newspaper articles. You know that? Not even in the write up on *Just InJustice*. What do you make of that?"

"Means they didn't want the public to know. Means they knew the killer prolly still had the bat."

"But they had you. You didn't have the bat."

"Ain't you listening? They got the wrong man. They knew it, and they didn't care."

The silence stretches long and heavy. "Nobody came forward after your folks put up the reward?"

"Oh, lots of people came forward, but they just wanted the money. They didn't have nothing."

But I do. If nothing else, I know a person who might be the unknown specimen.

My hand stretches across the table, touching his. I open my mouth, on the verge of telling him that I have the bat, when the guard taps on the table with his stick.

I jerk back, but Holt doesn't move, just stares down at the spot where I touched him.

When he looks up, he says, "I destroyed their lives by being at that party. Mom asked me not to go, said she had a bad *feeling*. She always thought she had a sense about stuff. Maybe she did." He pauses, and his full lips compress then pull tight in a grimace.

"You can still get your life back." I glimpse something gentle hiding deep within the depths of his eyes despite his own admission that he's "done other things."

"So you think she'll want to write something about me?" He looks from me to his hands, like he's self-conscious, speaking like a normal person. I wonder if the punctuated speech is part of the show, part of the mask he wears to keep others at a distance. If he's calculating enough to alter his speech patterns, he may not be as simple as I thought.

"I think she might." I shrug, in too deep to stop the lie now.

"My sister's the one you need to talk to. She has all the information." When he looks at me, I know he didn't kill Dietz. The rim of his eyes pool with tears, and he blinks to dispel it. Suddenly, the giant who stooped through the door is replaced by the awkward and unsure kid he must have been.

"She really believes in you."

Holt leans in, talking about his sister, about the website, about all the work she has done to try to find the real killer. He talks like a man who needs to fill the air. A man who has been starved of attention and conversation for too long. Before I know it, I'm pulled along with his every word, noting the way the enunciated words have dropped as if that was part of the story he was telling. But when I look up at the clock, our visit is almost over. I haven't done what I came here to do.

"Do you remember a guy named Chase Reddick?"

He nods, his whole body in on the action. "Sure. I knew him."

"Was he there that night?"

"Prolly."

"Did you see him?" *Yes. Please say yes.*

He shakes his head. "I don't think so—unless he was one of the damn snakes."

"I need you to think about it really hard." I lean forward. "I can't talk to your sister again. I can't do anything. But I'm telling you that somebody needs to run Chase Reddick's DNA against the unknown sample. But you can't talk to the Aldrich Police."

He does not speak. He looks confused.

"Have your sister tell somebody at *Just InJustice*. Tell your lawyer. Do something."

"What do you know about it?"

"That bat is in my basement, and I'm married to Chase Reddick. You understand? It can't come from me."

"Time's up." The guard taps his stick on the table, and we both jump to our feet.

"Why are you doing this?"

"Because I'm probably next on his list." I turn toward the door and walk through it without looking behind me. There is no going back now, and I feel powerful having confessed my suspicions. For the first time since Carmen died, my soul is clean.

I am infected by a sense of triumph as I leave the prison lot. Chase may kill me, but at least somebody knows him name. He will not get away with what he has done.

# Chapter 40

After driving back to Cartersville, I spend the afternoon fulfilling my alibi, using Chase's credit card to shop. Once I retrieve my phone from Dillard's, I head for the parking lot to plug it in. Six missed texts are waiting for me.

I text, *Sorry, I dropped my phone at Dillard's. Had to retrace my steps. Heading home.*

No dots appear, but the text shows it has been read.

My stomach churns as I drive down State Route 37, through the foothills that lead to the mountains where Carmen offered me cheap rent and an escape all those months ago. The stark rock edifices that rise along the left side of the road make for a narrow shoulder. I never like driving this closed-in stretch of road. After braking for a curve, the shimmy from earlier becomes a vibration. I focus on the steering wheel, gripping it as if I can will the motion to stop. The road is smooth enough. No need to panic. But I'm not in the ruts.

*Something is wrong.* I slow to pull off, but at fifty miles an hour, the right front tire jettisons off the vehicle, and my momentum stalls. The car spins, wrenching my hands from the steering wheel. Suddenly, I am facing the wrong direction. The oncoming traffic screeches and swerves, and I can't even scream. I close my eyes, my foot pressed to the floor as the car spins.

The crunch of metal sets my voice free. Through the windshield, I see the rock face coming at me as the car skids. A vehicle slams into the rear right panel. The airbag explodes. My scream drowns out the impact as the car jolts against the guard rail. My head jerks forward into the airbag. Powder fills my open mouth and lungs.

A second impact rocks me against the deflating side airbag, and my head crashes into the glass. It is chaos, the hiss and squall. Then the smoke settles.

The engine is dead. Sound stills, and my scream wavers to silence. I try to open the door, but the metal is twisted from contact with the guardrail. Blood stings my eyes. I close them as the pressure inside my head expands.

Everything stops. My breath freezes in my chest, my heart pauses the sluice of blood in my veins. Time stretches. I release one hand to move the gearshift into park, and my foot presses the emergency brake to the floor. My hands clamp again on the steering wheel, braced, waiting.

I do not know how long I sit. Eventually, my heart hammers in my chest. My breath rasps, filling my lungs again and catching on its way in and out of my throat. My arms and legs are rigid. My head pushes back against the headrest. Lights slide over the car. A form looms beside my door, and I jerk. *Chase?* The scream in my throat whispers out in a gasp.

He pulls at the handle, but the door will not open. I am so tired, exhausted, and I turn to watch him as he moves to the back door, which opens without difficulty.

"Are you okay?" When he speaks, some distant part of me registers that it isn't Chase.

"Can you move? What happened? Can you move? Are you hurt?" A long list of questions passes from his lips, but I have no answers.

"Unfasten your seat belt." He has said it several times, but I can't seem to unclench my hands from the steering wheel, and my head is on a swivel.

The seat belt is the only thing keeping me safe. The darkness narrows, and I let my eyes fall shut. The car rocks as he climbs into the back seat.

"Paramedics are on the way. Just stay with me." He fills the space in the car, and his breathing moves the hair off my face. I think I know him, but when I try to find his name, I can only see Chase.

A GREAT RENDING OF metal wakes me, the sound announcing the opening of the driver's-side door. The wash of air sets a shiver running through my body.

Hands reach in, grabbing under my arms. My muscles quake as I am pulled from the car, lifted, then laid on a stretcher. Moments slip. The man who was in my car is gone. Paramedics are in my face, shining lights into my eyes, asking questions.

*How did I get here? What is happening?* My mind stutters and falters, and I feel jerked through time, hearing the questions asked of me that I am unable to answer.

*My car was fine. It was fine.* Then I remember the small shimmy as I drove toward Dorrell.

I should call Chase to let him know I've been in an accident.

Lights flash in my eyes. More questions are asked, but I have no responses. My jaws constrict and clamp. My head throbs. Every muscle in my body aches. My mind loops, and I lose the thread of my thoughts as they load me into the ambulance. Panic arcs. The confined space is like a coffin, and I struggle against the straps securing me to the stretcher. Sometime later, I am aware of motion as sirens wail somewhere far away.

# Chapter 41

My nose is broken. Dark bruises spread across each cheek like a raven's wings in flight, but I've survived worse. I don't know if they've called Chase, but I spend the night alone in the hospital.

Early the next morning, the police arrive. It's not the Aldrich Police but two officers from Cartersville. The older officer with a thick Southern accent sits in a chair at the end of the bed and introduces himself.

"We just have a few questions for you, ma'am." He flips a notebook open in a casual way.

"Why did my tire fall off?" I ask, having a few questions of my own.

"It looks like the lugs were loosened on the front. The rear seemed unaffected."

"But how?"

"I'd say it was prolly tampered with. We see that now and then, mostly with bigger cars—gas-guzzlers that the zealots think are destroying the planet. Don't see it quite so often on smaller passenger vehicles, though." The cadence of his speech is like the ebb and flow of the tide.

"Why?"

The officers exchange a look. "You have anybody who would want to see you hurt?"

I blink twice. "No. Nobody I can think of."

"Can you tell me where all you went yesterday?"

"I was at the mall. All day."

A furrow creases his brow, and he places the end of his pen into his mouth. "Now, are you sure about that?"

"Of course I'm sure. I was Christmas shopping."

"That's interesting." He gestures toward his partner.

The younger officer steps forward to show me a grainy printout of my car passing under one of the surveillance cameras entering the lot. It is time-stamped 9:54 a.m. I hold the image as he presents me with another. It captures my car leaving the lot through a different gate, stamped 10:23 a.m., and I am confident that the other two images capture my return around three and my departure around five.

I have lost control of my face. Muscles spasm as I whisper, "You can't tell my husband."

"You go off to meet a boyfriend?" The older officer asks as I shove the photos back at his partner.

I shake my head. "You *can't* tell my husband," I whisper, just a little louder.

"Can't tell me what?" Chase's voice is as calm as I have ever heard it.

Panic floods me at his sudden appearance, and I draw in a shaky breath. The older officer seems to notice, and we make eye contact. I do not know what he sees in my face, but he takes a long second before he looks from me to Chase.

They make brief introductions before the officer explains, "Delilah here was just worried about us telling you that somebody tampered with the lug nuts on her car. Do you know anybody who would want to hurt your wife?"

Chase pushes his bottom lip out and shakes his head. "Nope." He turns to look at me. "Why would you be worried about that, honey?"

"I don't know." My mouth is dry, the saliva tacky on my tongue. "You're just so protective. I didn't want you to worry that I parked in dangerous area. You know how I never notice those things."

"That's true. You never do pay attention." He holds my eyes, and I cannot look away until he turns back to the officers. "Tell me about the lug nuts."

"Both front tires were tampered with. Left side was missing three nuts, and the right side obviously lost all. Allowed the wheel to come off."

"Anybody else injured besides my wife?"

"The man in the vehicle that hit her has minor lacerations, a few bruises, but nothing significant," the older officer says.

I cringe. I hadn't even thought about other people involved.

Chase smiles, turning on the charm. "Well, that's lucky."

"Yes. Lucky," the young officer agrees.

"Well, come on, Mark. We'll let this nice couple have some time." Then to me, he says, "We'll look through the surveillance at the mall, see if we find anything suspicious. Who does maintenance on the vehicle?" When I don't answer, he turns his attention to Chase.

"Monty's in Aldrich handles most things." Chase steps toward me and places his hand on my shoulder.

"Well. We'll be in touch."

They shake hands, and I go invisible on the bed, my muscles twitching. They could have shown him those photos, and I'd be a dead woman. Having an affair would be a safer alibi than the truth.

Chase is restless, pacing my room after they leave. He walks down to the nurse's station three times, trying to get my release finalized. In the bathroom, I change out of the hospital gown and into the jeans and sweater he brought. When I finish, Chase stands with a chair to wheel me out in, talking with a nurse.

"Where is Jackson?" I ask as I sit, glad he isn't here to see me like this. Butterflies in my stomach bat their wings against my heart.

"He's at school. He has a game tonight."

At first, I don't understand. Then I realize he wouldn't have been able to play if he missed school. "Of course. I wouldn't want him to miss that."

I balk at getting into the truck, but when no other solution for getting me home presents itself, I force myself into the passenger seat beside Chase and strap on the seat belt. I feel small in the cab, too small, and I imagine myself bouncing around inside like a pinball. Chase rests his arm over the back of the seat, his fingertips grazing my shoulder. I fight the urge to shudder at every touch. We do not speak.

We stop at the tow yard to collect the gifts I bought and my purse. The man has placed everything into a big trash bag, and I am relieved that the voice recorder and the notebook are not visible when I look into it.

I draw the bag closed as Chase tries to take a peek. "Gifts." I didn't use the recorder when I spoke with Dabney Holt, but the notebook is full of my theories, and I do not want Chase poking around inside. I reach in and retrieve my purse before tying the bag closed.

"Was this everything?" I ask the attendant, feeling the strain of speaking.

"Yes, ma'am. Cleared it myself." His teeth are stained with tobacco, and a thin stream of spit trails from the corner of his mouth to his chin. "You're welcome to go and look."

"No, I'm sure this is everything." I turn to walk toward Chase's truck.

"Actually, I'd like to see the car." Chase takes the bag from me and holds it with one hand.

The man nods, and we follow him out to the lot, where my car sits with other impounded or damaged vehicles. The scrape along the driver's side looks like a gash, like a suicide attempt, bleeding silver. Chase drops the bag of gifts to the ground as he makes his way around the vehicle. The damage at the opposing ends makes the car look totaled. A small tremor begins in the pit of my stomach and radiates out into my limbs.

"I'll have Monty's come by to pick it up tomorrow, see if it can be salvaged." Chase shakes hands with the man.

"That'll be just fine."

He flips a card from his pocket. "Send me the bill for the tow."

"Yes, sir."

Chase adds pressure to the hand on my back, and I step forward, allowing him to guide me from the damaged car through the lot and out to his truck. He drops the trash bag into the bed and goes around to the driver's side.

It takes me a full minute to force my hand to open the door and coerce my body into the seat. My teeth clench, and my muscles spasm as I fasten the seat belt. *I can't get phobic about cars now*, my mind hisses. But I'm afraid it's already too late.

When we get home, Chase ushers me up to bed.

# Chapter 42

A week after the accident, I drive the rental to the grocery store with a list for Christmas dinner. Chase will pick Geneva up at ten. I've used all of her recipes to plan the meal. That means days of prep because everything has to be from scratch. I am in the produce aisle, inspecting sweet potatoes, when a man's voice says my name.

"Ms. Stone?"

I look up. He seems vaguely familiar. "Yes?"

"It's good to see you up and around. How are you feeling?"

My memory clears at his accent, and I recognize the older officer from the hospital. He is not dressed for duty, although his close-cropped hair and upright carriage is a giveaway. "I'm better. Thanks for asking, Officer..."

"Glenn. Just call me Glenn. Do you have a minute? That we could talk?"

I push my buggy beside him as he leads me to the small coffee shop at the front of the store. He chooses a table. I leave my buggy at the perimeter, and my stomach flutters.

"Did you find something out about my car?"

"Yes." He leans forward. "We got an image of a man messing with your car at the mall."

"Who was it? Did you catch him."

"Unfortunately, we couldn't identify him. He's tall—six feet, maybe six-one—but he kept his face hidden."

Confusion fills me. I was certain it was Chase, but he's five-ten at best. "That's unfortunate."

"Yes, ma'am. But I wanted to talk to you about where you were."

My stomach flops, and fluid floods my mouth. For a horrible second, I think I am going to be sick. The wave passes, leaving beads of sweat in my hairline. "Why? What does it matter?"

"Who were you visiting at Dorrell?" he asks in his Southern drawl.

"Uh." Chills shoot down my spine, and I sink into the chair before I lose my balance.

"You can speak freely. If you'd be more comfortable, you can come down to the station. Who were you visiting at Dorrell?"

Carmen's lie blooms in my mind. "I was working with Carmen as part of the advance team for her aunt—she's a writer. She was interested in the Michael Dietz murder." My lips tremble, and tears spring to my eyes.

"You met with Dabney Holt?"

"You knew already?" I'm unsure if I speak the words or only mouth them. Of course they would have been able to track me. I had to put in my driver's license number at the prison.

"We spoke with Mr. Holt. He says that you may have information about that case. I assume that is why you didn't want to tell your husband. Would you like to tell me about that?"

I nod. There is nothing else I can do. My breathing is shallow, sporadic, and the field of vision narrows until I have to put my head down. *Breathe.*

When I look up, the officer is looking patiently at me. "Just to be sure that I'm on the right page, when you say Carmen, you are speaking of Carmen Fuentes, yes?"

"Why are you here? Are you following me?" My voice is little more than a whisper.

"I could have come to your home, but I thought a chance meeting might be... safer for you."

I push my hand through my hair. *What is happening? What does he know about Carmen? What does he know about Chase?* Understanding dawns. He has spoken with Holt. He knows about the bat in my basement. *Did Holt tell him that I thought I'd be next?* He has figured out the dance—the dirty little secret that Chase and I have hidden from the world.

He blows out a breath, reaches in his pocket, and unfolds a sheet of paper. It is a photocopy of an artist's sketch. My hand flies to my mouth. It's Chase.

"Do you recognize this man?"

I hold his eyes, unable to do more than blink in acknowledgement.

"This came through the wire shortly before you had your accident. This person was seen leaving Ms. Fuentes's apartment the night she died." He folds the paper and slides it back into his pocket.

I close my eyes, and a single tear breaks through. It feels like minutes pass before I am in control enough to look at him again.

"What do you know about Michael Dietz?"

"His bat is in my basement," I whisper across the table, terrified that the words are out of my mouth and cannot be put away. Terrified that I've not spoken loudly enough for him to hear.

"Do you believe your husband killed him?"

I nod almost imperceptibly. "We were trying to put the pieces together."

"You and Carmen?"

"Yes." Weight lifts from my shoulders, and I sit up straighter. *He won't get away it.*

"We can move you to a safe house if you are in danger, ma'am." He touches my hand, and I look at the point of connection, remembering the expression on Dabney's face when I touched him. I understand what he felt, to be touched by someone with a promise of sanctuary.

Of course I am in danger. I have lived my entire adult life in danger. "I can't leave my son."

"We can move him with you."

I shake my head. "Geneva's coming for Christmas." It's insane. It is not a reason to stay, but she looks forward to Christmas so much that I can't take it from her like that.

"Well, if you're sure."

"He has friends in Aldrich." I add, "Police." I need to get up and away from Glenn. Somebody might see me sitting here with him and have questions. "I have to finish my shopping."

"Yeah. Thank you for your time, Ms. Stone. We'll be close."

I reclaim my cart and pick up my list, scratching through sweet potatoes as if I haven't been interrupted. When I look back at the table, Glenn is gone. For a moment, I wonder if I imagined the whole thing.

# Chapter 43

Christmas morning dawns with fresh snowfall layering the lawns. The breakfast casserole is already in the oven. Chase's big gifts put mine to shame. He bought Jackson the new Xbox he has wanted for months and even surprises me with a silver cuff bracelet and a heart-shaped pendant on an eighteen-inch chain. My meager offerings, a sweater and a new wallet for Chase, jeans and an Under Armour jacket for Jackson, are quickly forgotten as the two of them head upstairs to set up the Xbox in Jackson's room while I clean the mess from the packages.

A knock makes me jump, and I turn to look out the window. Two police cars are parked in front of the house.

*Oh my God, they're here. They are really here.* The realization crashes down on me. Glenn was real. What he said was *real.*

My stomach flops. "Chase!" I call up to Jackson's room.

When I open the door, an unfamiliar officer greets me.

"Can I help you?"

"We have a warrant to search this property." He hands me an envelope, but I don't open it.

"Oh. Of course." I stop myself from pointing the way to the basement.

"Is your husband home?"

I call for Chase again, and he comes down the steps as I usher the officer into the house.

Chase freezes at the base of the stairs. "What is this?"

"Mr. Reddick?"

"Yes?"

"We have a warrant to search your properties." The officer turns and motions to the rest of his team, who brush past me at the door.

The momentary surprise on Chase's face disappears. He strolls over to me and plucks the warrant from my hand.

The officer gives him a few seconds to look it over. "If you'll step outside of the house, sir."

"Sure thing." He obliges as if he hasn't a concern in the world. "Can I ask what this is in reference to?"

"Mr. Reddick, I'll need you to come to the police car with me."

Jackson comes down the steps. "What's going on?"

I shake my head at him, still feeling like it is all too good to be true. "I don't know, honey. They want to talk to your dad."

Following an officer, Chase steps past me with his back straight and his jaw clenched. He doesn't look at me. As he is walked out of our home, the chaos that has lived inside of me settles to silence.

We follow him onto the porch but stop as he goes down the steps. "Dad?"

He doesn't respond, just walks down the sidewalk. Finally, he turns to face us over the roof of the police car as the officer opens the door for him. To anyone else, the look on his face might be unreadable. It turns my blood to ice. Rage sets his features to stone. We lock eyes before his head dips below the line of the cruiser, and he slips inside.

Jackson and I are permitted to gather our coats and shoes before we are escorted out of the house. We stand huddled together as the snow falls.

Bruce is on his porch, watching. He comes down his steps and speaks with an officer, who nods. Bruce calls out to us, "You can come over to my house. No sense in you freezing to death!"

The last thing I want is to step into Bruce's house, but Jackson is demanding answers that I won't give and nobody else has. I need to get him away from all this. We move toward the old man across the street, my teeth chattering. I turn to see Chase in the squad car. His face is forward, his back straight. Jackson is almost hysterical.

We watch from Bruce's house as boxes are carried from the basement and loaded into an evidence van. I bite my lip when an officer comes out with a plastic bag containing the bat.

From this angle, I think I can see Michael Dietz's initials carved into the wood.

# Chapter 44

From Bruce's front window, we stand witness to Chase's arrest. Though I do not hear the charges, I recognize "murder" and "Carmen Fuentes" on the officer's lips as he reads Chase his rights.

Bruce steps onto the porch. "Don't worry, son. I'll call Curt Shelnut. He'll fix it. You just don't say a *thang,* and it'll all be okay!"

That's exactly who Chase called after Jackson was expelled, and the framework of enablers, and my placement within that structure, is suddenly clear. Bruce doesn't even know what he is being accused of, and he is offering absolution.

I pace the old man's living room until the police finish their search of my home, and we are permitted to return. When I enter the house, the telephone is ringing.

"Hello?"

"Delilah, this is John." John has been Chase's right-hand man for years, and if Chase has anybody that he would call a brother, it is John. "What's going on? We were heading out to my in-laws' and saw the police at the office. Has something happened? Did we get broken into?"

"No, nothing like that. Chase has been arrested."

"What? What for? What the hell did he do?"

"I don't know. They haven't told me anything." His mentioning of in-laws makes my stomach sink. *Geneva.* I must tell her what has happened. The clock on the microwave glows 9:07 a.m. She'll be expecting Chase to pick her up at ten for Christmas lunch. "I'll let you know when I find out something."

After changing out of my pajamas, I explain to Jackson that we need to meet his grandmother. He would rather stay in his room and lick his wounds and come to terms with his new reality in private, but he is docile as we head out to the rental car. I don't want him to be there for this conversation with Geneva, but I don't see what other choice we have. It's too much of an imposition to send him to Dalton's on Christmas. We back down the drive and into the street and see Bruce in his window.

"I could ask Bruce to come over while I'm gone so you wouldn't be alone."

"I'm old enough to be home alone, Mom. I do it all the time."

"Not today. Okay?" We lock eyes, and he nods.

I leave him sitting in the car and rush to Bruce's porch. He sees me coming and meets me with an open door.

"I have to go see Geneva. Jackson needs some time. I just wondered if you could be in the house—" My voice breaks, and tears slide down my face. *What have I done to my son?*

Bruce pats my shoulder and agrees to keep an eye on him.

I rush back to the car, swiping at my face. "You can stay. Bruce is on his way."

Right behind me, Bruce crosses the front of the car, lightly tapping twice on the hood with a fist.

"Thanks, Mom." Jackson holds my eyes for a split second before getting out and walking up the stairs to our porch.

As I idle at the bottom of the driveway and watch them enter the house, my phone rings. Curt Shelnut informs me that Chase has been arrested for the murder of Carmen Fuentes.

"I don't know what the evidence is, but that's what the arrest record says."

"That's crazy," I whisper. It's exhausting pretending that I don't know what's going on, and I'm still worried about Jackson. A tear rolls down my cheek. "That was a suicide." *I knew Carmen would be the one to take him down.*

"I don't know. But I'm heading to the station to meet with him. You may want to be there."

"No. I have to tell his mother. I can't come."

He doesn't answer for a second. "We'll need to talk about my retainer."

"Of course. We'll do that, but I can't let Geneva find out on the news." I put the car in drive and pull forward.

"Okay. I understand. I'll call you after I've met with your husband."

GENEVA IS WAITING FOR me where Mrs. Tillman used to greet me. She passed away at the end of November, and my weekly visits have been sadder without her. Her anticipation of some date that probably happened seventy years ago convinced me that love could happen, not for me, maybe, but for others. He must have been a great man for her to be so excited for their next meeting.

"You're late!" She looks down at her delicate wrist, annoyed. "Why are you here?" Chase had promised to pick her up on Christmas. I know she is disappointed that I've come instead of him.

"Something's happened." I sign the guest registry and guide her into an alcove where we will have a degree of privacy. "I don't know how to say this, but..."

"Just say it. Is Chase okay? Is it Jackson?"

"Jackson's fine." My heart hurts. Tears come as I imagine how I would feel if somebody had to tell me my son is not who I thought he was. There is no way to soften it, and Geneva is a straightforward woman who doesn't tolerate hemming and hawing. "Chase has been arrested."

"What for?"

"Murder." I squeeze her hand, wishing I didn't have confirmation from the attorney because I don't want to be the bearer of such news. It's better that she learns it from me, though, so I press forward. "They came and searched the house and took all sorts of stuff out of the basement." They took the bat, so that means they might link him to Michael Dietz as well. "I don't know all the details, but his attorney is meeting with him now."

"That's bull. That's just bull." She puffs her cheeks and blows out. "Chase is a good boy." She looks away from me as she says it. Geneva knows better. She has seen my bruises, and while I never admitted anything to her, I wonder if her husband hadn't sometimes stressed his point with a fist.

When the details of that morning are all laid out, we sit and contemplate the future.

"I'm sure this will all just work out. It must be a mistake. You just have to keep things together until he can get home to you."

Like I want him to come home.

"You got to run the business now so you can pay for the lawyer."

I put my hand to my temple. "I hadn't even thought about the business."

She tuts. "I never did understand why you didn't step up. I never would have let somebody else keep Vern's books. It was our company, and we passed it over to you. You should have done your part."

Her words feel like a slap. "Chase didn't want me there."

"You should have just stood up and told him how it was going to be. Because look at you now. You don't know what you need to know." Her sympathy evaporates, and the litany of my failures sits just beneath the surface. Geneva and I have been friendly, but I have always known that she thinks I am weak.

"I better go. I don't want to leave Jackson too long."

"Yes, yes, poor boy. What are we going to do? You go home. Be with Jackson." She wrings her hands and places her cane in preparation for standing. “You get him a good lawyer. Get my son the best lawyer you can find.”

“Yes, ma'am.”

# Chapter 45

After leaving Geneva, I drive to the police station where Chase is being held. I park next to a car with the license plate ShelntI and wait. Chase's attorney said he needed a retainer, and I have my checkbook. It's just an excuse to have a word with him. I need to know exactly what my husband is being charged with.

I sit for ten minutes before the guy belonging to the car comes out. He is stout and solid like a college football star. He swaggers to his car, and I open my door and call to him. He halts in his tracks then comes around to shake my hand.

"I'm Delilah, Chase's wife. How is he?" I don't really care, but it's what I feel I must say to get the information I want.

"He's upset. He's confused about how this happened. Says he didn't do anything wrong."

A wry smile compresses my lips. Chase always has a good reason, justification for what he does. No evil person thinks they are in the wrong. "What do they have against him? What are the charges?"

"Let's talk in my car." He opens the passenger door for me. When we are sheltered from the risk of being overheard, he continues, "They've booked him on the murder of Carmen Fuentes."

"How do they know it wasn't a suicide?"

"I won't have all the information until I get discovery." He pulls out a folder and flips it open. "But from what I've put together from the autopsy report, the ligature around her neck was inconsistent with hanging. It was a straight line, suggesting forcible strangulation."

The scene blooms in my mind against my will—him overpowering her, her fighting, knowing the cost if she loses. But Chase whips her around, tossing the cord around her neck with his free hand. His knee is pressed into her back, pinning her down as he pulls the cord tighter.

It's too much. I blink, and the scene evaporates. I have to keep it together in front of the attorney until I know Chase can't get out of this. "How do they know it was him?"

"They found tissue under her fingernail and ran that through a DNA database." He scratches the back of his neck. "Funny thing is, it triggered a match to an unknown sample in an old case. That put Carmen's killer at the scene of that other murder too."

"Did the DNA match Chase's? How do they know it's him?" I ask again.

"Still waiting on the lab results. But they had an eyewitness at Fuentes's apartment. The next-door neighbor gave a description of the man she saw leaving the building the night before Carmen was found, so they made the arrest."

*Glenn's sketch.* It wasn't perfect, but the artist had captured something of Chase. She'd thought he was a new beau, but he was rude when she greeted him. *Serves him right.*

"They've linked the two cases but still didn't have a true lead as to his identity." He keeps talking, but I can fill in the rest. I had the accident—*was that attempted murder?*—Glenn came to my hospital and recognized Chase, and the ball started to roll.

"It doesn't look good, I'm afraid," he finishes.

"He didn't deny killing her, though, did he?"

"Of course he said he didn't do it. Has an alibi." He reaches out and touches my hand, as if he thinks he is reassuring me.

"Me? *I'm* his alibi?" Rage warps through my veins. *Never again.*

He nods enthusiastically like the victory is already his. "We'll put you on the stand, destroy the eyewitness, explain his DNA some other way."

"I cannot go on the stand."

"No, it's fine. The prosecution can't force you to testify against your husband, but you can certainly testify for the defense."

"You don't understand. I won't do it."

Puzzlement marches over his features. "But you're his alibi. You have to testi—"

"I'm not. Chase wasn't home. He was not with us." My words come out in a pitch lower than normal but controlled. *He is not going to kill my best friend, the only person who* ever *knew me, and then try to use me as his alibi.*

The attorney opens the slim folder again and scans his notes. "Are you certain?"

"Positive."

"He seemed confident that he was."

"Maybe he could use his girlfriend, Bridget Dietz. She might be willing to give him an alibi, but I doubt it."

"Dietz?"

A hoarse laugh escapes me, but I no longer care what Curt Shelnut thinks. If I'm the only thing between Chase and life behind bars, I can finally step aside. "Did he not mention her? Michael's little sister, whom Chase hired to work in his office."

"No, ma'am. He did not." His jaw twitches.

"Let's be clear. I think he did this—all of this—and I hope he rots in jail for the rest of his life. Now, I've brought my checkbook. I'm happy to settle your retainer if you still want to work on his case."

To his credit, Curt Shelnut appears to think about it for a moment before accepting my check. I leave him in his car, and as I am backing out of my spot, I see him walking back through the station door. Apparently, I've given him something to talk about with his client.

# Chapter 46

"All rise."

The prosecuting attorney, Chase, and his defense attorney stand like they are connected at the hip. The rest of the courtroom follows.

Today is Chase's first appearance in court, when the judge determines bail. We are sitting behind Chase, although I do not think he knows we are here. Curt Shelnut, the son of Preston Shelnut, who apparently "goes way back" with our neighbor Bruce, leans toward Chase to whisper instructions. The attorney catches my eye and gives a curt nod but does not speak to me.

Jackson puts his hand in mine like he is a child again as the legal teams identify themselves and then Chase as the defendant. The first-degree murder charge for the death of Carmen Elizabeth Fuentes is read.

The prosecutor stands and says, "We have evidence that links the defendant to the death of Michael Dietz. We are interviewing witnesses in that case."

"What charges do you expect to bring?"

"First-degree manslaughter, Your Honor."

Chase sits stoically, unmoving, and I bite my tongue to keep control of my face. Suspecting he had something to do with Carmen's death isn't the same as having it confirmed by someone else and seeing the undeniable evidence. For the first time in his life, Chase will have to go on the stand for what he has done—the ugly truth he made me feel crazy for believing.

Squeezing Jackson's hand, I glance over at him. His face is all hard lines, his eyes downcast. My heart sinks. Somehow, I believed I could destroy his father without also destroying him. If only I had run away to the mountains the way Carmen had suggested. Instead, I set all of this in motion, and now she is dead, and my son will never be the same.

The prosecutor's voice cuts through my thoughts. "Though the prosecution is still reviewing the Michael Dietz murder, the current evidence indicates the defendant's motive in Ms. Fuentes's murder." He points at Chase. "Chase Reddick became aware that Carmen Fuentes had discovered evidence that he had murdered Michael Dietz, and Mr. Reddick, in cold blood, plotted to kill her to keep her silent."

Jackson tightens his grip on my hand, and I lean against him, grateful that he is here, even though I am torn about the damage it will cause. I probably should have warned him, but I couldn't find the right time, and everything is moving so fast. The words flow over and around us. I caused this. I put Carmen in danger. I have damaged my son.

*No. Chase did this.* He did all of this and more. He killed Carmen, he killed Michael Dietz, and he probably tried to kill me with the car. I sit straighter in my seat. I will never cower again.

"Given the brutality of these cases, the State contends that Mr. Reddick would be a flight risk. He has substantial resources—"

"Your Honor, that's unreasonable!" Curt Shelnut launches into a well-rehearsed speech about Chase's strong ties to the community and his family.

I hold my breath, unable to fathom the chaos of him coming home. But this time, we wouldn't be there. There is no way I would let him near me again. I believed he was capable of murder, but knowing it changes everything. I will no longer be his victim.

The judge does not hesitate. "Bail is denied. Chase Reddick will be remanded to the Shandy County Jail until his arraignment." The gavel falls.

Chase is removed from the courtroom. Jackson and I wait in case he turns to look, but he walks out without seeing the confusion on Jackson's face or the determination on mine. Another case is called, and a different defendant rises. Jackson nudges me, and we make our way out of the courtroom during the transition.

"Ms. Stone." The name hangs heavily in the air. "Ms. Stone, could I have a word?"

Officer Grant stops beside me, and I nod.

"How are you holding up?"

"As well as can be expected. You remember my son, Jackson."

Officer Grant is part of the enemy camp. The way he was chummy with Chase when he came to my home, questioning Jackson about that stupid drawing, still makes me sick. He can't be trusted.

"Yes, ma'am." He reaches out and offers his hand.

Jackson hesitates, but then he surprises me and shakes Officer Grant's hand. *He's becoming a man.*

"Could you come by the station? I'd like to ask you a few questions."

"I don't have anything to say."

"Ms. Stone, it might be in your best interest to speak with me, to tell me what you know."

I look at Jackson. "I don't know anything, and I can't be forced to testify against him," I say for Jackson's benefit. I don't know all the rules about spouses testifying, but it seems to be in line with what Shelnut said. Even though he never wanted me to take his name, he still married me.

"Well, as a point of fact, you could be asked to testify about anything you know about Michael Dietz. You weren't married when that murder happened."

"I don't know anything about Michael Dietz."

A deep crease furrows his brow. "Come by my office, Ms. Stone." He compresses his lips, and I feel the fray of uncertainty at the back of my mind. I can't be the one who set everything in motion. Jackson might never forgive me if he knew I set out to destroy his father.

"All right. I'll come by." It is what it is. We all have to pay for the choices we make.

# Chapter 47

"What was that all about?" Jackson asks when we are in the rental car.

"I don't know."

"Did Dad do what they say he did?"

My heart breaks for him. "I don't know."

"Please tell me what is going on!" he shouts, making me flinch.

"Okay. Let's just get home. Then we'll talk." We drive in silence for a few moments before I say, "You know I loved your dad, right?"

He stares out the window and does not offer words.

"He's a little *intense* sometimes, right?"

He rolls his eyes, clearly frustrated by my treating him like a kid.

"You know he has a temper?"

He blows out a breath of air, and when I glance at him, he says, "Yeah. Like he's a door."

"What do you mean?"

"Oh, I ran into the door," he says in a falsetto voice. "I tripped up the stairs." Suddenly, I understand, and my face flushes in shame. "I know he hits you. I've known since I was, like, ten. I'm not stupid."

My instinct is to deny it, but I compress my lips and let the truth stand. "Your father is a violent man. That's why I was so upset about Heather."

He nods but doesn't speak.

"You okay?"

"Did he really kill Carmen?" When Jackson was small, he called Carmen "Auntie Car," but when he hit puberty, he dropped the endearment. It was a sad transition for both her and me, but we let it stand.

"I don't know," I say because I do not have all the facts.

Jackson doesn't say anything, but his frustration is palpable.

"You were in the courtroom," I say. "You know what they think."

"Mom. Do *you* believe he killed her?"

Then I understand. He is seeing me. He is reframing everything he has ever thought he knew about me. "Yes. I believe he did." My chin puckers, and for moment, I fight to regain control of my face.

Jackson gives me time as he stares out the window. Then he asks, "Who is Michael Dietz?"

"He was a kid we went to high school with. He was kind of a low-level drug dealer."

"They think Dad killed him too? Why?"

I don't dare to take the easy road. He deserves to understand why this is happening. "From what I've been able to put together, they were business partners, so to speak. I didn't know that about your dad's business when we met, but Dietz was killed in some kind of drug-deal-gone-bad scenario."

"Dad was a drug dealer?" He is appalled, lit up by the unexpectedness of it. He can imagine his father being violent, but Chase dealing drugs seems to have shattered everything Jackson knew about his father.

"I didn't really know your dad when we were in high school. It was just my senior year that I went to Drake. You know, after my mom died. I didn't know Michael, either, but I remember seeing them both around school." I remember Birdie calling her brother Mikey, and my heart pulls for her. She must be putting the puzzle together like Jackson. I can't imagine what she must be feeling about Chase now, the way this will shake her reality.

"I got to know your dad when we were in college. You know this story." He nods, and I turn down our street. "I was infatuated."

We park in the garage, but neither of us make a move to leave the car. I release a long sigh and tell him about the night that Chase came back into my life. The air is motionless when I tell him about seeing Chase coming from the bathroom, about the wet spot on his shirt. "He had looked... just, well, wild. But I still had that crush on him, so I told the police we had been together all night. Then we moved to New York."

"You lied to the police?"

"No. Not really. We were together all night, from the moment he came up to me, and I didn't know where he was before that. I never imagined he could have hurt somebody. They arrested somebody else for that, and he's still in jail. Although that may change, I guess. I never thought your dad had anything to do with that." I can't bring myself to say "murder." "He never talked about Michael Dietz, and I was so busy the weeks after that, I wasn't paying attention."

"Dietz," Jackson says as if a chord has been struck.

"What?"

"That's Birdie's last name."

I nod. "She's his sister." I don't know how much more I can tell him without causing him to lose his center.

"You knew that?"

"She mentioned him at Thanksgiving, so yeah. But I still didn't put everything together."

"But they were..." He stops and turns and looks out the window.

"What?"

He shakes his head and reaches for the handle. "He killed him and then hired his little sister. And they—" He looks at me with wide eyes, apparently catching himself. "Anyway, that's fucked up."

"Very." I agree without even reacting to his language. He isn't a kid anymore. If he wants to use a vulgarity to express himself, this day has given him that right.

"I thought your dad may have had something to do with Michael when we were driving home on Thanksgiving. He asked what Birdie said to me. He was annoyed that we talked. I told him that she mentioned that her brother died."

"Dad said he'd been beat to death with a bat." Jackson turns to face me.

"I didn't think you were listening." I look at him, surprised. He was in the car, but he had his earbuds in. I wonder what other delicate conversations he's heard because we thought he wasn't listening. "That's what he said. But I was doing some research about it but didn't remember seeing that information anywhere in the newspapers. They just said 'blunt object,' which could be about anything."

"Why were you researching it?"

"Oh, um... Carmen's aunt is a writer. We thought it would be an interesting story if we could put together some details for her." The lie trips off my tongue, and I am grateful that Carmen gave me this excuse all those months ago.

We linger by the car for a long minute. He knew that Birdie and his dad were having an affair. That's what he started to say. It feels like a betrayal to think he knew and didn't warn me. I draw a long breath then let it escape. But, in his defense, I couldn't imagine having to tell a parent something like that.

"Now the police want to ask me what I remember about the night he died, and I don't know what I should say."

"Just tell the truth." He frowns and pulls the door open. When I follow him into the house, he heads for the stairs. "I'm going to my room."

"Are you okay?"

He stops and stands on the fifth step for a long second before slowly turning to face me. "It's just... a lot to process. I need some time."

I hear it in his voice, and I see it in his face. Everything that was child in him has evaporated. I watch his ascent long after he disappears into his room.

# Chapter 48

Weariness forces me off my feet, and I let the bones of my back go liquid against the couch. My eyes scan the room, still upheaved from the police search. Pictures are shifted on the mantle, papers rifled through on the desk where the computer monitor sits like a decapitated head, missing its CPU.

Dread fills me when I remember that I must let Geneva know the results of the initial appearance. Not only did the judge deny bond, but Chase wouldn't even look at us. There's no more pretending that I am on his team. Just before Christmas, we had visited Geneva together, the picture of a happy family. Even though the regular visits were left to me, Chase fussed over his mother. It was actually quite sweet. *She's going to be so disappointed.*

Sleep takes me. When I wake up, I am covered in a blanket, and the smell of coffee brewing is coming from the kitchen.

"What's this?" I ask when I find Jackson at the coffeepot.

"Thought you'd need it. You've got to talk to the police today." Jackson's smile is weak around the edges, but he pours me a cup and leans against the counter.

I wrap my hands around the mug, drawing strength from its warmth.

"I texted Dalton. He says I can come over. I really don't want to go to the police station, and I figured you wouldn't want me home alone."

I nod, grateful that he has thought ahead.

"WHAT CAN YOU TELL ME about the night Michael Dietz was murdered?" Officer Grant stares at me from across the interrogation room table. My secret phone is sitting between us. The box filled with my research—the same one I tripped over at the flip house and later found in our basement—is on the floor beside a black duffle bag.

"I didn't know anything about it at the time. I was at the Warehouse with my friends. I saw Chase from across the room, and he came up to me to talk."

"You were acquaintances?"

"We had dated for a short time, three years before. I was heartbroken he ended it. When he approached me again, I was flattered."

"You stated that you and he had 'been together all night' when interviewed by police."

Back then, Chase was nonchalant about going to the police station, confident that I would play my part. I served him well.

"Yes, sir. When he came up to me, we were together for the rest of the night. We left together and went back to his apartment."

"What time was it that you first saw Mr. Reddick at the Warehouse?"

"I don't know. My friends and I left the dorm at seven and walked to the square, so we probably got to the Warehouse around eight-thirty, maybe nine."

"It took an hour and a half to walk to the square from the university?"

"No. We stopped at the Downtowner for a bit, but it was really crowded, so we moved on. We weren't in a hurry. We ended up at the Warehouse because it was less packed." I shake my head. "It may have been closer to seven-thirty when we left the university. It was a long time ago."

"Then what happened?"

"After he came up to me?" I ask, and he shrugs, just wanting me to tell the story. "We flirted. We drank. A lot. Then we left the bar and went back to his apartment."

"You came out the door of the bar, which faced onto the street. Did you make note of anything happening at the house across the road?"

"We didn't go out the front. We went out a side door, into the alley. I saw the lights, maybe the ambulance. But we were rushing, kind of. I don't know." I've spent a lifetime filtering my words and don't know how to speak without doing so. "I do remember the ambulance. I saw them wheeling the boy out. Chase told me not to look over there. He wanted to get back to his apartment. We'd had quite a bit to drink."

He makes a note about the bar's side door. "Did you stop anywhere along the way?" They hadn't asked that question the first time.

"Well, paused, I guess. He picked up a baseball bat in some bushes." This new information should be the nail in the coffin. It could put Chase away for long enough that I can create a new life, maybe even long enough for our son to figure out how to forget him. That is, if Officer Grant does his job. I still don't know what he'll do with my testimony.

He taps his pen on his notepad. "Where were the bushes?"

"Just at a house a couple of blocks from the square." I could probably take him there, but I don't know the exact address. It's not like it matters. There wouldn't be evidence of the bat after all this time.

"The bat was in the bushes? Could you see it?"

"No, I couldn't. He knew it was there. At the time, I figured it was his—that he had left it." If only I'd understood the bat's importance then. Maybe the trajectory of my life would have been different if I'd mentioned it the first time I spoke to the police.

"Did you notice initials on the handle?"

"No. Not then. But the bat was in our basement."

"And you saw the initials on it then?"

I nod. "I thought it was M.O. or O.W., but now I know it was M.D., I guess."

"Did you think it was strange that he kept a potential murder weapon in the basement?"

"No. I never thought it was a potential anything. It was just a bat."

Dabney Holt's words echo in my head: *"It was just a fuckin' bat. What is there to tell? It was yea long. Made of wood."*

"You didn't think it was odd that he kept it?"

"You play softball with him, Officer Grant. Is it strange that he would have a bat?"

"Why did you tell Dabney Holt about it? What made you think this was the bat used to kill Dietz?"

Of course he knew I spoke with Holt. He must've told them what I said. I look down at the box on the floor, and comprehension washes through me. *They know everything.*

I let out the tension I've been holding. "It started because my husband left me a note. It was a long time ago, but he wrote that I was an 'alibi.' It always stuck with me, that word. Why alibi? He could have said I was a 'rebound' or a 'booty call' if he had just wanted to hurt me. Then I started thinking about the night he came back into my life, how it felt like a foregone conclusion that he was going to New York with me, how he just took over. I guess I put the two things together. Then, when I was researching Michael Dietz, I never saw the murder weapon called a bat. It was always an 'unrecovered blunt object.' But one day, Chase mentioned Michael Dietz was killed with a bat."

Grant draws in a long breath and leans back in his chair, his hand behind his head, studying me. "When was that?"

"Thanksgiving."

His brows furrow. "Carmen Fuentes was dead by then. When did you first start looking into Michael Dietz's murder?"

"In August. Maybe September."

He leans forward, his eyes intent on mine. "So you and Carmen Fuentes conspired against your husband?"

"I don't think that is accurate. I asked her to keep my research because I didn't feel it was safe to keep it at my house."

"Could you identify your research for the record?"

"Yes." I indicate the box beside his bag of tricks. "It has my high school yearbook. You'll find that note inside it and a bunch of copies that I made at the newspaper office about the Dietz murder and Dabney Holt's trial. That's pretty much all there was. I'd hit a dead end because I couldn't go to the police. Carmen didn't like that, and she arranged to meet with Scott Young, who worked the Dietz case, but she was killed before the meeting."

"When was that meeting scheduled for?"

"Friday, the day after she was killed."

He makes a note, and I wonder if that was new information.

"Why did you think you couldn't go to the police?"

I give him a level stare. "How is your mama, Officer Grant?" He looks confused, so I drop the imitation. "Chase has friends on the force."

"So you and your friend were trying to take Cha—your husband down." Grant catches himself on Chase's name, but he doesn't acknowledge what I've said.

"In theory, I guess. But I don't think either of us ever thought anything would come of it. It was just research. Something for me to focus on until the next—" I start to say "beatdown" but bite my tongue. "We wanted to put together a proposal for her aunt to write about."

"How is your relationship with your husband?" Officer Grant leans back in his chair.

"It's complicated. Chase seems like a good man. You know him." I lower my eyes. "I mean, he's not perfect, and I try him sometimes. But he thinks he's a good man. He tries to be." I put my hand to my eyebrow scar but drop it when I see his eyes following my motion.

"Do you recognize this book?" He slides a black-and-white composition book out of his bag and places it on the table.

I shake my head. "No."

"Were you aware that Carmen Fuentes kept a journal?"

"She used to when we were in college. I didn't know she still did." My fingers itch to reach across the table and gather the book. These are the only words left of Carmen.

"Do you remember the night of August thirteenth of this year?" He opens the journal while I troll through my memories, looking for August.

When I don't answer, he looks down at the page and reads: "*D came over today. C had beat the shit out of her, and she couldn't even tell me why.*" He slides a loose sheet of paper across the table. It's a photograph blown up on a sheet of printer paper, displaying my damaged face in full color. I do not remember her taking it, but I don't remember much from that particular day. "I assume D is Delilah, and C is Chase? Would that be correct?"

"She said he was gonna kill me." My words are barely audible.

"Would you like to tell me about that day?" For the first time during the interview, there is a hint of kindness in his voice.

"I can't remember it." I meet his eyes and quickly look away. "I mean, I remember being at Carmen's and Chase calling me. He was right out on the street." I give a hysterical laugh. "He *always* knew where I was.

"Carmen didn't want me to go back with him. She wanted me to run away, but I couldn't leave my son, and Chase would never let me go if I tried to take him." My voice breaks, and I'm minutely aware of the shift in his expression as he takes in my words. "He promised... he promised things would be different. Said we could go to counseling."

"Did you go?"

I drop my eyes. "No. There was never a good time." I am careful. I don't know how much Carmen had written about my plan to take

Chase down. "He was busy with work, and everything was better. We've been better since then."

Officer Grant sighs, then we sit in silence for a long minute. "When you went home with him, you had an idea that he may have had something to do with the Dietz murder?"

"In a vague way, yes, but I don't think I ever thought I'd be able to do anything with it. I think I was just keeping myself occupied."

"Until he beat you again?"

I meet his eyes and refuse to look away. "Is there any chance he's getting out before the trial?"

"You were at the bond hearing. He's in till the trial. He's been booked on suspicion of the murder of Carmen Fuentes, and we are reviewing the Dietz murder. He'll have an arraignment, probably Monday. I assume you will be there?"

Curt had called me after the bond hearing.

"Listen, Chase doesn't want you and Jackson coming back for any more court appearances. In light of everything, I expect you'll understand. He was insistent that I tell you that and encourage you to abide by his wishes."

"How am I supposed to know what's going on?"

"I'll talk to the court," he said. "See if we can arrange a feed."

I want to be there. I want to see him destroyed piece by piece. But it's better for Jackson if we aren't present. I'm lost inside my head, but Grant clears his throat and brings me back to the present.

"Chase asked that we not be present. I respect his wishes."

Grant nods, but his forehead creases.

"We have son. We have a business that we have to keep operating. If Chase doesn't want us there, we'll do the part that we can."

"Delilah, look..." His voice is soft, and I glance up to see him studying the photograph Carmen took. "I know it might feel too late, but we can help you. You can still press charges for this."

*Help* me? In his extension of an olive branch, I feel like I'm being seen for the first time. "Do you think I should?"

"If I were you, I would. The more they have against him, the less likely he will be released. We can also file a restraining order in case his bond appeal is granted.

"Okay." Chase already knows I've defected. It's not like I can do more damage by making it official.

"Let me grab some paperwork. Do you need anything to drink?"

I look toward the door, ready to get out of this stuffy room. "I'd take a water." I settle in to fill out the report against Chase, plowing on. It's going to be a long day. When I finish here, I still have to meet with John, who is running the business for the moment. I text Jackson to let him know I'll be delayed. I feel like I've been gone for too long already, but he is with a friend, so I try to relax.

# Chapter 49

The house is silent and empty when I pull the truck into the garage. I enter through the kitchen and call out, not expecting an answer, knowing by the stillness in the air that Jackson is not upstairs. The sound of a bass line is absent. I pull out my phone and check for messages. The last one was from him seven hours ago. *Heading to Dalton's. Love you.*

He hasn't responded to my text about being a little longer, but it shows delivered. They are probably playing basketball or video games, so it doesn't matter. This is exactly what Jackson needs—a friend to stand by him, to make him feel normal in this crazy time. I say a silent prayer of thanks for Dalton.

I reread his text. The "love you" makes my heart swell. We are going to be okay. We'll get through the trial and see what comes next. We'll leave Aldrich and go someplace where nobody knows us, where we can start over. *I wonder where Jackson would like to live.*

I call him, but it goes directly to voicemail. I pull up Dalton's mom's phone number and dial. "Hey, Claire. Thanks for letting Jackson come over today."

"What do you mean? Jackson isn't here."

My eyebrows furrow. "No, he is. He was coming over to hang out with Dalton. Did they go somewhere?"

"No, he's not here. Let me check with Dalton." She turns away from the phone to yell for her son. "Do you know anything about Jackson coming over?"

In the background, I can hear Dalton clearly. "No, I haven't seen him today. We talked last night, but I haven't heard from him since."

I blink, unable to process this new information. "No, he has to be there," I say into the receiver. "I have a text from him that says he was on his way."

"I'm sorry, Delilah. He never came over."

"Then where is he?"

"I have no idea."

"I had to go talk to the police today. I couldn't take him. He said he arranged to spend the day at your house." When the words are out, I sense I overstepped or overshared, like my dirty clothes are hanging on the line. But I don't care. This must be a mistake. If Claire would just look around, maybe Jackson would suddenly appear. "Are you sure he isn't there?"

"I'm sorry, but he really isn't."

"Okay. I'll call him." I hang up and dial him again, leaving a message this time. "Jackson, where are you? I talked to Dalton. They haven't seen you. Call me back. You're scaring me."

I run up the stairs and push through the closed door of his room. It's like stepping into a display. The bed is made, the desk cleared. The floor has vacuum marks. It feels like I've stepped into an alternate universe where my son keeps a tidy room. I open his closet, and the empty hangers clatter on the rod. I open his drawers and see that they are picked through.

My stomach plummets. *Did somebody come into my house and take him?* My mind races. *But why clean his room?* I call his name as I rip apart the house, searching the closets and the basement. There's no sign of him in the yard, either, so I rush across the street and knock at Bruce's door.

"Did you see Jackson today?"

He shakes his head. "What's happened?"

I explain as best as I can that he was supposed to be at a friend's house, but he wasn't there. They hadn't been expecting him.

Bruce shrugs. "I wasn't watching."

"Oh my God, Bruce, you are always watching! Where is my son?" I shout as if he is somehow responsible.

"Sit down," he says with enough force that the hysteria recedes.

I don't sit, but I do stop shouting.

"Would he have run away?" he asks.

"No. He's only fourteen."

"Kids run away all the time. Have you called the police?" I shake my head, and he says, "That's probably the first place you should start."

FOR THE SECOND TIME in a week, the police search my home, this time looking for signs of struggle. They ask me to recount the morning with Jackson, and I tell them how he made me coffee and said he was spending the day at Dalton's.

"Found a note!" An officer makes her way down the stairs, holding the paper by a corner with gloved fingers. "Recognize this?" She holds up his phone.

My mind hollows as the officer lays the note and the phone on the table. I try to make sense of the two opposing details. Jackson loves his phone. He is tethered to it—he wouldn't leave it on purpose, but he left a note that suggests he made a choice. I stare for a long moment before any of the words he has written make sense.

*I'm sorry. I just have to get away from here. I'll be okay. I got to start my own life. I'll let you know when I get settled. I'll never be like him. Don't worry. I'm not a baby anymore. I can take care of myself. Love you. –Jack.*

# Chapter 50

The moment in Carmen's bathroom, when she suggested that I leave my son and start a new life somewhere else, plays on repeat in my mind through the long hours of the night. I'd considered it—I may have even wished that I didn't have him so could I run, but it was never something I really wanted.

There's nobody left to call. I wish for Carmen. Sick as it is, I wish for Chase too. I even wish for my mother, who I lost so long ago that I almost can't remember the sound of her voice. When I cannot stand the house any longer, I step outside, and the bite of the air takes my breath away. *Is Jackson out in the cold night, or has he found shelter?*

Bruce's light is on in his living room, and he calls out the door, "You okay?"

Mute, I nod then wave, not wanting him to shout across the silent midnight street again. I go back into the house, clutching my phone in case someone finds Jackson.

Minutes tick by, and at two in the morning, I finally sit, too exhausted and weary to pace any further. I plug the phone in and hold it, willing it to ring. After I spoke with Dalton's mom, I called every one of his friends. Most were kind, but a few were cold. The perception of our perfect family has changed, and I suddenly understand Jackson's need to leave town. My eyelids grow heavy with no end in sight to this nightmare.

At 5:12 a.m., my phone trills and startles me awake.

"Hello?"

No response comes from the other end of the line, but I can hear breathing.

"Who is this? Jackson?"

"Did you know?" A woman's voice, quaking with emotion.

"Who is this?" Fear washes over me, and for a moment, I think it is Carmen, calling from beyond the grave.

"Did you know that he—that he killed my brother?" She breaks and sobs.

The cobwebs recede in my brain, and I heave a sigh. "Is Jackson with you?" Birdie was the one person I hadn't thought to call. *He likes her. He may have gone to her when he felt overwhelmed.*

"Answer me. Did Chase kill Mikey?"

"I don't know." I feel as shattered as she sounds. Something breaks, and I sob and push my hand through my hair.

We do not speak for a minute, then she says, "Why did you ask about Jack?"

"I can't find him. He ran away. It's too much. It's just too much." The desperation to escape this moment in my life makes me think that I understand how somebody could take their life, how Carmen could have thought that ending the momentary pain would be worth a cord around her neck.

Only, she didn't. She didn't commit suicide.

"Can I come over?" Birdie doesn't wait for my answer. "I'm coming over. Okay. Okay? I'm coming over."

After she disconnects, I drop the phone, and my body sways as that moment in Carmen's bathroom haunts me. *I wished him away.* Guilt flows through me like lead. I did everything wrong.

All I can do is wait at the window for Birdie to arrive. She walks up the steps like a pretty bull, determined. I open the door, and we stare at each other, the oddness of the situation dawning. That I would turn to Chase's mistress for help.

Birdie breaks the silence. "Tell me what you know."

"I don't know if he killed—"

"Not about that. We can't do anything for Mikey. Where is Jack? Why did you think he'd be with me? Why isn't he here?" She does not move, just stands in front of me with so much grief on her face that it's like I am seeing myself reflected.

"Come in."

As she follows me into the living room, my words fall out in a tangled mess about his note and what happened yesterday. When I'm empty of them, I sit down on the sofa and drop my face between my knees.

"Where do you think he's gone?" She lifts a photo of him from the mantel.

"I have no idea."

"What are the police doing? We need to get out there and look for him. Go take a shower. We're going to the police station."

I stand and stare at her. I appreciate the lifeline but feel that the air between us is toxic. "I know you were sleeping with my husband."

Her lips pull, and she looks like she might cry. She nods. "I stopped, though, after I met you. It was a terrible thing to do. I'm so sorry." It is no excuse, and she has to know it is not enough, but the apology is anchored in pain.

"Did he ever hit you?"

"No. God, no." The horror is evident in her face, and she draws her hand to her neck as if she needs to push her heart back into its proper place.

"At least he kept something just for me." I head up the stairs, unsure that I have said the words, but the loose edge of something in my mind is shifting, churning. If I do not pull it together, I will lose myself.

"Oh my God. Delilah, did he hit you?"

I stop on the landing and turn to face her. Drawing my upper lip into my mouth, I realize I cannot say these words. Not at the police station. Not to Jackson. And not now. The shame is too great. I close my eyes and turn away.

Birdie tilts her head and looks up at me sadly. “Go take a shower. I’ll get coffee started. Then we’ll figure everything out.”

She is not my friend, but I am grateful she is here, and maybe, just for today, I’ll forgive her.

# Chapter 51

"How did you hear about it?" I ask when I find her in the kitchen.

"Morning paper." She pours a cup of steaming coffee into a mug.

Up until today, the papers had only mentioned the arrest of a suspect in connection with the death of Carmen, and they didn't release anything about Michael Dietz. The full story printed this morning, the Monday after the holiday.

"It was on the local news Saturday night," I say, barely a whisper. It was terrible, watching them put Chase's mugshot up next to a picture of Carmen. It felt sensational, and they hinted that they were having an affair, which they did not mention in the following report, as the details began to fill in around her.

"I don't watch TV." Birdie hands me the mug.

The shower helped, and I feel less hysterical in clean clothes. My hair is damp, pulled back into a messy bun. The small, fractured hinge in my mind is more connected. I sit at the table, too weary to stand.

"Tell me about Jackson. When did he leave?" A small collection of photographs sits in front of her, taken from the now-empty frames around the room. She makes notes as I walk her through the timeline. He has been missing for nearly twenty hours, assuming he left the house when he sent me that last text.

"I tried to call him on my way over, thought he might pick up," she says.

I nod. "He likes you quite a bit. But he didn't take his phone."

"What? Are you sure he ran away?"

"He left a note, told me he'd get in touch when he got settled."

Toast pops, and Birdie jumps up to grab it. She slides the plate across the table to me. I look at it for a long minute before scraping butter onto it.

"Does he have anybody he would go to?"

I shake my head. We don't have people, me and Chase.

"And the police aren't doing anything?"

I shrug. They said they would search, but I don't know how much effort they will put into a runaway.

"Well, come on. We need to spread the word, get you in front of as many cameras as possible."

THE COFFEE AND TOAST fill some of the void inside of me as Birdie drives us to the police station. By nine o'clock, Officer Grant has me standing beside him in front of a crowd of reporters. He looks at me. "Ready?"

I nod.

He faces the reporters. "Thank you for being here. Around quarter to six yesterday evening, we received a call about a missing teen, Jackson Reddick. If anybody has information about his whereabouts, we ask that you come forward. Jackson is fourteen years old, five feet, eleven inches tall, with dark-brown hair and eyes. We will not be taking questions, but his mother, Ms. Stone, would like to make a statement."

Attention shifts to me. I clear my throat and step up to the podium. "Jackson, please come home. We love you. I love you. Please let me know that you are okay." I feel ridiculous, but this is what Officer Grant suggested I say. He does not want the press conference to turn into a feeding frenzy about Chase. Birdie brought Jackson's most recent school photo, which I settle on the podium so the reporters can get a good look.

It is over so quickly that I feel pulled through time. But Officer Grant's format doesn't stop the onslaught of press questions.

"Does the boy have a history of violence like his father?"

"What's the connection to the Dietz case?"

"Does Chase Reddick know his son is missing?"

I'm escorted from the room before I have a chance to react.

# Chapter 52

My phone rings as we reach Grant's office. Waterstone Manor flashes on the screen. A wave of guilt passes through me. I do not have the strength to have a conversation with Geneva. Before I can face her, I need Jackson to come home. I haven't been able to go there since before Chase's hearing. Her long fingers and the slant of her smile appear in my mind, but the blue of her eyes is sapped away, suddenly fading to gray. A sick feeling grows in my stomach.

Jostled by the image, I stare down at the screen. It's the administration number, not Geneva's personal line. "Hello?"

"Mrs. Reddick?"

I don't bother correcting her. "Yes?" I push my shoulders back, trying to release the tension building at the base of my neck.

"I'm calling with some unfortunate news. Your mother-in-law..."

"What?" I close my eyes, trying to find the strength to make the trip to Waterstone to sit and talk her through everything. I should have gone yesterday, but there hasn't been time. There are no words about Jackson that I can comfort her with.

"I'm afraid she's passed away, ma'am."

"What do you mean?"

"She appears to have had a fatal heart attack. The paramedics came right away, but she has a DNR. I'm so sorry for your loss."

"I don't understand! When? Where was she?"

"About an hour ago, in the common room. I called you first thing. According to the other resident, they were watching TV when the incident happened."

My mind warps as I see the press conference flashing across the common room screen. "Oh," I whisper, and tears flood past my lashes.

"I'm so sorry. We all just loved Ms. Geneva. We are heartbroken." I nod and manage a muffled sound before she continues, "We do have some paperwork you'll need to sign, or your husband... I guess you would probably need to come by."

"I'll do that."

Geneva died of a broken heart. I hadn't even thought about how the press conference would affect her. I should have called, but the hours since I realized Jackson was gone are like the blink of an eye. She loved Jackson more than she loved anybody else.

I hang up and turn to Officer Grant. "I need to see Chase."

Grant nods. "Is everything okay?"

"His mother died."

"WHAT THE FUCK IS GOING on?" Chase shouts when he is escorted into the visitation room. His hands are cuffed, but I doubt it's enough to keep him from killing me with so much anger burning through him. "Where is Jackson? You've lost my son?"

"How do you know?"

"We have a TV. It's not like it's Alcatraz."

The guard doesn't leave, and I keep my distance. Grant is still processing the restraining order and my complaint. Chase makes his way to the table and sits. He sinks low in the seat, insolent.

"Where have you looked?" He lists off several of Jackson's friends, and I shake my head until he finally stops.

"We'll find him," I say with more certainty than I feel.

"You better hope so."

"We'll find him." I clear my throat and look up at the camera mounted on the wall. "I'm not here about Jackson."

"Then why are you here? Remorse?"

It's like a slap, a punch. "What do you mean by that?"

"Was it worth it? Everything it cost you to get away from me?"

My mind reels. "I don't know what you are talking about."

He shrugs and folds his arms across his stomach. "I can't say I blame the boy for leaving you." He runs his tongue over his teeth as if speaking with me leaves a foul taste in his mouth.

"Your mother is dead."

His mouth drops open.

"She had a heart attack, Chase. *You* did this—this is what you get for killing Michael Dietz, for killing Carmen. For trying to kill me. Everybody knows what you are now. Your son had to get away from what you've done, and your mother couldn't bear to live with the truth of what you are. Everybody sees your stripes."

I turn on my heel, and the guard allows me out of the room before Chase can speak or rise. For once, I get the last word.

# Epilogue

I file for divorce on Tuesday, the day after Chase is arraigned for the first-degree murder of Carmen Fuentes and second-degree manslaughter of Michael Dietz. I put the house on the market and hire movers to pack the furniture for storage.

Geneva is buried without ceremony or celebration. I cannot stop crying. It's not fair that Chase has brought this evil into our lives. The weight of loss and sorrow is too great to bear. The sadness is like an anchor dragging me into the sea.

It takes two weeks to put together a contract for John and Melanie to buy out my share of the business, and I give them a good deal to be Chase's partners. John is still on team Chase, and I wonder how long it will take him to see Chase's true colors.

I read on the *Just InJustice* blog that Dabney Holt has been exonerated, his conviction vacated, and that he has been released from prison. The idea that something positive came from the ruin makes me smile for a moment, but it isn't enough to drag me out of the sea.

Glenn comes by the house as Birdie, my unlikely ally, is helping me pack my belongings into a U-Haul.

"Ms. Stone," he calls from the street, and I want to rush to him, hug him, thank him for seeing me, for recognizing Chase in the artist's sketch.

"Hey! Good to see you." I set the box down, and we stand on the sidewalk.

"Moving?"

"Yeah. It's time to start my life." Jackson's note floats through my mind. "What brings you by?"

"We've been going through the surveillance footage at the mall from the day you had your accident, and I wondered if you might take a look." He withdraws two folded sheets from inside his jacket, in much the same way he withdrew the sketch of Chase all those weeks ago.

The first one shows a man in a gray hoodie, kneeling at my front tire. His back is to us, and he is unrecognizable. I turn to the second page and see the man getting into a truck. It's grainy, but the hoodie has slipped back, and the face is clear.

"Do you recognize that man?"

"I do. That's Tom Lassiter. That's Chase's best friend from high school."

He nods as if he already had the name and just wanted confirmation.

Birdie has stopped packing and comes to stand beside me.

"You aren't moving far, are you?" Glenn tucks the pages back in his pocket, out of sight.

"Not far. I've rented a cabin up in Blue Divide."

"All right. Don't change your number."

"I won't." I can't, because Jackson is going to call me someday, and it's the only number he knows.

"Any word on your son?" Glenn asks as if he's read my mind.

"No. But he'll come home. He needs some time."

"I'm sure he will. All right. I got work to do." He tilts his head and saunters across the street to his car. We watch until he drives away.

AFTER BIRDIE AND I finish loading the U-Haul, we drive up the mountain, neither of us speaking as we leave Drake and Aldrich behind us. The weight of all that I have lost crushes me the farther we get, and I love Birdie for not trying to fill the silence with useless words.

Blue Divide is quaint, with hiking outposts and canoe rentals, a restaurant, and a smattering of cabins and homes through the woods nearby. The cabin I'm renting isn't the one that Carmen promised me so long ago, but I think she would like that I finally found my way to the mountains. I try not to fixate on the chain of events I set in motion by poking around about Michael Dietz. Yes, she would still be alive, and Jackson probably wouldn't have run away. I did what I did, and I can't change it. The price was too high, but it's been paid. Now all I can do is put one foot in front of the other and try to make her death count for something—and wait for Jackson to call. The cabin is small and has two bedrooms, for when he comes home.

Time stretches. Days roll in and fold over each other. The seasons are harsh on the mountain. The nights leave frost on the pine litter at the edge of the trees.

Bundled in blankets, I sit on the back porch and watch the day rise through the fog of my breath. Behind the cabin is a stream, which Jackson will love. It's only about ten feet wide, but it fills the house with the sound of water running over rocks, and that makes me feel the weight pressing in a little less. The locals say there is good fishing in the creek. I sit at the small kitchen table and watch the day fall to dusk. Hours are lost waiting for my phone to ring, waiting for Jackson to call and say he's coming home. I do not believe he is dead. He will call when he is ready. One day, he won't be mad about everything that we put him through.

I take a job in a diner called the Blue Gazelle. I fill a lot of coffee cups, and nobody knows my history. My name tag says Sue. I have locked Delilah away with my past to keep her quiet. Sometimes, I forget myself and find my smile when somebody comes in and calls a greeting, "Heya, Sue. What's cookin'?"

I like the people who live on the mountain, but the nights at the cabin are longer and darker than anything I have ever known. When the weight crushes me to the bed and I wake feeling Chase's hands around my neck, I pace the floors, haunted, checking the locks and the windows.

My feet ache from the hours at the café, but some nights, I find sleep. Every morning when I wake, I check my messages and add one to the count. It has been seventeen days since I last heard from him. Then twenty-three. On the sixty-second day, a text pops up from an unknown number.

*Hey, Mom. How are you?*

# Acknowledgments

Writing is not a solitary process. So many people go into the making of a book. Of course, Lynn McNamee at Red Adept Publishing tops the list. She saw potential and helped hone it. Special thanks to Jessica, Marirose, and Sherri, who made up my editorial team, and Erica, who had the right vision to create the cover. Without them, this book would have been less than complete.

As always, I thank my family. My husband, Jeff, and our kids—Kyle, Olivia, and Isabel—are the greatest cheering section I could imagine. Without them, I would be lost. My parents, Donna and Nick, gave me a solid foundation and helped me understand that life is complicated and everybody has a story.

My friend Amy, who heard probably a hundred different plotlines as this novel was taking shape, thanks for being my sounding board so I could work through the minutiae.

To the team at Hometown Novel Nights (www.hometownnovel.com), thank you for your dedication in connecting local authors with readers in our area. I never dreamed my community would be so full of amazing writers.

And most of all, I have to thank the woman who spoke with me, very candidly, about her life trapped in the cycle of abuse. That conversation was the impetus for this novel. By sharing her fear and survival with me, she planted the seeds for Delilah finding her voice. Though I don't know the ending of her story, I think of her often, hoping she has found her way out.

## About the Author

Angie Gallion has been a stage actor, an anti-money-laundering investigator, a photographer, and a paralegal. She has lived in Illinois, California, Missouri, and Georgia and has traveled to Greece, the Dominican Republic, Scotland, and Ireland. Angie dreams of traveling the country on wheels with her husband once her children are grown. She is currently rooted outside of Atlanta, Georgia, with her husband, their children, and their two French bulldogs.

Angie's writings usually deal with personal growth through tragedy or trauma. She explores complex relationships, often set against the backdrop of addiction or mental illness. Her first novel, *Intoxic*, was the 2016 bronze medalist in the Readers Favorite for General Fiction. That book was a twenty-five-year adventure in self-doubt and hesitation.

Read more at www.angiegallion.com.

## About the Publisher

**Dear Reader,**

**We hope you enjoyed this book. Please consider leaving a review on your favorite book site.**

Visit https://RedAdeptPublishing.com to see our entire catalogue.

Check out our app for short stories, articles, and interviews. You'll also be notified of future releases and special sales.

Made in United States
North Haven, CT
25 October 2024